D0959182

*A Christmas Deliverance*

# A Christmas Deliverance

### A Novel

## Anne Perry

BALLANTINE BOOKS • NEW YORK

Published in the United States by Ballantine Books,
an imprint of Random House, a division of
Penguin Random House LLC, New York.

BALLANTINE is a registered trademark and the colophon is a trademark of
Penguin Random House LLC.

LIBRARY OF CONGRESS CATALOGING-IN-PUBLICATION DATA
Names: Perry, Anne, author.
Title: A Christmas deliverance : a novel / Anne Perry.
Description: First edition. | New York : Ballantine Books, [2022]
Identifiers: LCCN 2022023110 (print) | LCCN 2022023111 (ebook) |
ISBN 9780593359105 (hardcover ; acid-free paper) |
ISBN 9780593359112 (ebook)
Subjects: LCGFT: Detective and mystery fiction. |
Christmas fiction. | Novels.
Classification: LCC PR6066.E693 C4653 2022 (print) |
LCC PR6066.E693 (ebook) | DDC 823/.914—dc23/eng/20220516
LC record available at https://lccn.loc.gov/2022023110
LC ebook record available at https://lccn.loc.gov/2022023111

Printed in Canada on acid-free paper

randomhousebooks.com

2 4 6 8 9 7 5 3 1

First Edition

Book design by Sara Bereta

To Harriet Emily,
and all who are new to this world,
and bring trust and joy with them

*A Christmas Deliverance*

"*A*re you going to stitch it?" she asked nervously, holding out a small, bloody finger.

Crowe guessed she was about four or five years old, and her eyes brimmed with tears that she was trying very hard to hide.

The finger was bleeding quite heavily. It would need stitches to hold it, and bandages to keep it clean as long as possible. This would be difficult with the cold and wet weather on the banks of the Thames, and even more so for a child with probably only a makeshift shelter to live in, and very little to eat. She had come to the clinic alone. She might have a parent, but probably not.

Most of the poorer people living on the riverbanks knew of Crowe's clinic, which catered specifically to their needs. He had opened it several years ago, after he had become skilled in healing, before he had officially qualified to call himself a doctor, or indeed to practice medicine at all.

3

Crowe never charged these people for his services. But they had no money anyway.

Not much had changed in the years since he had opened the clinic, except that he was now officially qualified. And he had gained the confidence to face authority and stand his ground. Occasionally now, on rare occurrences, someone could pay and Crowe would have enough for supplies . . . other than food.

"Are you going to stitch it?" she asked again.

He examined the finger. "Yes, I am," he replied.

She sniffed. "Can you darn it where the hole is?" she asked hopefully.

Crowe thought perhaps she had seen her mother, or her grandmother, darning the holes in a sock. "Not exactly," he replied. It was always better to tell the truth. When he saw how her eyes grew wide, he added, "I'll stitch it closed, and then you have to keep it covered and dry. It will fill in itself. You can do that." It was more hope than belief.

She nodded slowly.

"Now, hold still, and be very brave," he instructed. "Perhaps you don't want to watch. You don't have to."

She blinked and a tear ran down her cheek. She nodded, then watched as he cleansed the wound, and then chose a needle from the small case and threaded it with

4

very fine gut, almost like a hair. He had to keep his attention on what he was doing, so he was sure to catch the blood vessel, as well as the broken skin. He must leave her with only a slight scar, not puckered in a way that would always be uncomfortable.

She flinched as the needle pricked her, but she did not pull away.

Crowe worked as quickly as he could, only now and then looking up at her for a second or two. He knew he was hurting her. Fingertips were intensely sensitive, but there was nothing else he could do. The wound had to be given the chance to heal. If it became infected, she was too small, and perhaps too malnourished, to fight the infection off.

After the last suture was in place, Crowe trimmed away the excess thread and cleaned around the wound. Then he went straight on to bandage it, heavily. He reminded her not to take off the outer layers, even if they became soiled. "To protect it," he explained. "And now," he added, "I'm going to have lunch. Would you like some, too?" He knew she was probably hungry most of the time.

"I haven't any money," she said in little more than a whisper, as if frightened that he would be angry.

He smiled and gave a shrug. "Neither have I, as it

happens. So . . . will you have lunch with me? It's vegetable soup, with potatoes in it."

She gave the smallest nod, barely a movement at all.

"Come on, then. Can you eat with your left hand?" It was the right one that had been injured.

"Yes."

He led the way out of the room in which he and his assistant, twenty-two-year-old Will Monk, more often known as Scuff, saw their patients.

$\mathcal{S}$cuff, too, had begun as an orphan, when he was a little older than this child. Actually, he didn't know his birth date, or how old he was. He had spent his early childhood, after his mother had married his stepfather, scraping out a living as a mudlark, one of the small boys who salvaged items from the riverbanks when the tide was out: coins, metal screws, pieces of coal, anything that could be sold. Scuff had been befriended by William Monk, of the Thames River Police, and later officially adopted by Monk and his wife, Hester. In addition to not knowing his birth date or age, Scuff also had no idea what his given name was. But he did now: he was Will Monk.

Crowe still thought of him, and spoke to him, as Scuff.

Crowe led the little girl into the kitchen. Only Crowe and Scuff actually lived in the clinic, but very often patients who had been operated on remained here until they were sufficiently recovered to leave. There were quite a lot of food and medicines locked away. Some of the food was simple, like oatmeal, and there was always good red wine, particularly claret, something that restored strength and spirit in people not able to eat. And, to some degree, it dulled the patients' fear and pain. That, of course, was locked away. Things that did not keep, like bone broth, were consumed quickly.

There was also a very large stove, to provide lots of hot water necessary to launder stained sheets, or even blankets.

Crowe pulled the pan forward from the back of the stove. It was filled with a thick soup. It had been bone broth originally, but all kinds of things had been added, mainly cabbage stalks and potatoes, until it had become a meal in itself. He ladled out a serving for the child, and another for himself, then he placed the bowls on the table and indicated Scuff's chair for the little girl.

7

He looked closely at her. He watched carefully and saw that she looked mystified.

Crowe dipped his spoon into his bowl and then tasted carefully. It was a little hot, so he blew on it gently, then put it in his mouth, all the time watching her.

She copied exactly what he did, even down to blowing on the spoon, then carefully putting it into her mouth. Although it was a little too hot, she refused to show it.

Spoonful by spoonful, they finished everything in the pot. Crowe was more than full, but the child had eaten as if her legs were hollow.

They were just finishing when the next patient came in. He was a middle-aged man with a large, angry boil on his neck.

"Can you do anything about this, Doc?" he asked. "I got nobody else I trust to do it, an' I can't reach it myself."

"Certainly," Crowe responded, looking at the protruding, swollen mass. He could almost feel the throb of it and imagine the pain.

The child was transfixed.

"Can you help me?" Crowe asked her.

She nodded, as if too horror-struck at the idea to find words.

With quick, practiced hands, Crowe laid out two sharp knives, and several old, but freshly boiled cloths.

He directed the man to sit on one of the chairs, and then he spread a large piece of toweling around his shoulders, tightening his grip on the man's upper arm for a moment, to offer reassurance.

"Right," he said with confidence.

He had never asked the girl's name, so he had to get her attention by looking at her. "Will you pass me the blue cloth? Do you know blue?"

She looked puzzled, and then seemed to be ashamed.

"It's the color of the sky when it's sunny," he explained.

She passed him the right one.

"Thank you." He took it, rinsing it out in the bowl of warm water, and washing the angry boil. Then he gave it back to her. She put it down where it had been.

"Knife," he requested.

She had no trouble with that.

In a single movement, he cut the angry flesh and released the pus inside. Then he took the largest cloth and mopped it up. After this, he removed the remnant of the angry, bloody, and purulent mess and dumped it into the bin. He would burn the contents afterward.

"What's your name?" he asked the little girl.

She stared at him.

"I've got to call you something," he explained.

She looked puzzled, and then, again, embarrassed.

"Then I'll give you a name. There was a Queen Matilda once, a long time ago. How about Mattie?"

She nodded quickly.

"Right, Mattie, will you please pass me the cleanest piece of cloth on the table?"

She looked at all three pieces, and passed him the best one, looking at him shyly.

He took it and pressed it against the wound, where the boil had been, then applied two pieces of sticking plaster to hold the cloth in place.

"Don't get it wet, and don't get it dirty," he instructed the man.

"Is that all?" the man demanded dubiously.

"The dressing might need changing tomorrow. Don't use a cloth that hasn't been boiled clean," Crowe instructed.

He saw how Mattie looked at him. "What?" he asked.

She glanced away, thinking, and looked up at him only when she had found the words. "Mine, too?" she said tentatively. "Can I come back and have you do it?"

He realized with overwhelming pity that she probably had no access to a cloth of any sort, much less a clean one. He should have thought of that. He smiled at her. "Yes, of course, if you don't mind coming all this way?"

"I don't mind." She gave him a tiny, shy smile, then turned and went out of the door and into the street. And then she ran.

$I$t was half an hour later when Scuff returned with a heavy bag on his back. He was very different from the rather hesitant young man who had begun working with Crowe nearly three years earlier. He studied from books as well, which he found far easier to understand and remember after he had seen the reality. Everything he read was made that much clearer while watching Crowe perform the techniques and explain what he was doing. Buoyed by his newfound knowledge, and the confidence Crowe instilled in him, he was working toward the serious pursuit of medicine.

Scuff had told Crowe that his mother and her new husband had other children, and five-year-old Scuff had been put on the riverbank for longer and longer times, where they expected him to fend for himself. He had adapted to the change quickly, in order to survive, and this was when he became a mudlark. A few years later, there was no room for him at all at home and, effectively, he became an orphan whose life depended on his ability to scavenge.

So much of the maturity and growth of Scuff was thanks to William Monk. When Monk had first joined the Thames River Police, Scuff was around eight or nine, and they had met during one of Monk's investigations. It was young Scuff who had taught Monk the river wisdom regarding water, tides, and the people along the banks who made their living on what was called the longest street in London.

After a time, Scuff became part of William and Hester Monk's family. It was where he felt safe for the first time in his life. When it was time for him to choose the path his future would take, to everyone's surprise he chose not to go into the police like Monk, but into medicine, like Hester, who had been a nurse with Florence Nightingale in the Crimean War.

With Christmas less than two weeks away, Crowe knew many people would be thinking about the holiday, but he had no reason to. He had no one, whereas Scuff could think about the Monks, and what he could offer them as a gift.

For now, Crowe must focus on the clinic, and the

poor people who walked through the door in need of his services.

$\mathcal{S}$cuff nodded when he came in, placing on the kitchen table the supplies he had brought and must now separate and put away, reaching up to high shelves. While Crowe was tall and lean—well over six feet—Scuff was a couple of inches shorter, but quickly catching up with him. In appearance they were very unalike: Scuff was fair-haired and blue-eyed, the opposite of Crowe, whose eyes and hair were almost black.

The two men were also different in another way. Scuff felt safe with his memories, and he had a belief in himself that had only a few holes in it. William and Hester Monk had been good to him, supportive and loving. They were family. He had much to be grateful for. Crowe, on the other hand, kept the recollection of his many battles, his victories and losses, shrouded in silence. If he'd had family, nobody knew of them, and it was clear that he intended it to remain that way. For Crowe, life was about a future that one could change, not a past one could not.

Crowe set to helping Scuff unpack the supplies, which included a little food and a lot of bandages and medicines. There was also some claret, which they called "surgical spirits," for their patients.

Among the items was something that Scuff produced out of a brown paper bag, holding it up for admiration like a prize. "For Christmas," he said with a wide smile.

"Christmas pudding?" Crowe said in disbelief. "What did you pay for that? Who will have to go without?" He said that wryly. Funds were short and they were both painfully aware of it.

"I paid nothing," Scuff answered, putting the pudding at the back of the shelf and closing the door. "It was a gift from Old Mother Watson. It's not payment for anything in particular. Sometimes she just needs someone to listen." He stopped, looking at Crowe as if expecting a reprimand.

Crowe understood Scuff's expression. They had discussed the subject of time wasted on patients who had nothing medically wrong with them, nothing that could be treated. Scuff had insisted that all some people needed was a listening ear, kindness, and to be believed. Many people could deal with pain and the inconvenience it caused, as long as someone else understood.

Crowe understood and yet he preferred to concentrate on providing medical help, sometimes surgery. He had profound medical skills. Listening was for those who could not give answers, let alone get people to admit they needed help.

But it was Scuff who had survived alone on the river. He knew the culture of beliefs, regardless of the facts, and he found himself explaining these to the older and more clinically experienced Crowe.

Now he had brought a Christmas pudding for them to celebrate. But it was less than a fortnight until Christmas, and there was much to do before then.

They had few patients that afternoon, which gave them time to tidy cupboards and do a little laundry. There was an elderly patient Crowe knew he should visit to make sure he was taking his medicine, and to check that his infection was gone, or at least improved. He explained this to Scuff and then left the clinic.

Crowe walked the short distance. After seeing the man, talking with him for a few minutes, he walked back by a slightly longer route. Christmas was in the air, with bright decorations in windows, everything from handmade drawings of Father Christmas to flurries of tinsel tied to the base of some of the streetlamps. He told himself that he should be happy at this time of year, but this holiday brought home to him his loneliness. What was Christmas without a family? Or someone to love?

He found himself high above the river, where he could see the lowering sun shine on the mist covering the water. There were often lines of ships lying at anchor, waiting their turns to be unloaded. Through the haze, he could barely see the jagged black angles of the cranes and derricks along the dockside.

He had come this way because it reminded him of Eliza Hollister—Ellie—a young woman he had treated after a particularly harrowing accident. And for whom he still held fond memories.

From where he stood, Crowe had a view of large houses, trees carefully tended to in freshly dug winter gardens. These were not the homes of dockworkers, nor of the rather well-off importers and shippers. These grand houses belonged to the people who owned the ships, the warehouses, and sometimes the expensive cargoes as well.

Albert Hollister, Ellie's father, was one of the richest and most comfortable of them all. His house was huge, its massive stone façade just visible behind a garden of evergreen laurel bushes and professionally trimmed holly hedges. The house was filled with servants. And inside lived Ellie, whom Crowe had checked up on twice after her treatment.

Anyone walking past this home might see one of the gardeners trying to look busy when there was in fact nothing to do. There were no fallen leaves to pick up, because the last of them was long gone. The trees' branches were bare, a black fretwork against the darkening winter sky, and with a skeletal beauty of their own.

If someone saw Crowe, they would think him just another lanky figure loping along in the deepening shadows, a man wearing a long-tailed black jacket that flapped behind him. No one would recognize him here. These people did not require the services of a doctor who worked in a free clinic. That he had treated Ellie was a matter of circumstance: her accident had occurred very close to his clinic.

If he were walking closer to the water, however, and in the narrow streets that ran beside the river, there would be few who did not know him. Most of his patients were living there, some of them in a single room, or a lean-to offering little warmth and no running water.

Crowe pulled his mind back to Ellie, and the first time he had met her. It was in the spring, nearly a year ago. A young boy had come to the clinic, throwing the door open and crying out for help. There had been a serious traffic accident nearby. A light, privately owned gig had collided with a much heavier goods dray drawn by two Clydesdale horses that were twice the size and weight of the single horse pulling the gig. None of the animals was hurt, but the driver of the gig and his passenger were both badly injured and needed immediate help if they were to survive. The passenger was a young woman, Ellie Hollister.

Crowe had left Scuff, instructing him to complete the treatment they were in the middle of administering. Grabbing his emergency bag, which was always packed and ready for sudden crises, Crowe had raced after the youth, following him the short distance to the scene of the accident.

It was easy to spot: the broken gig lay in the road, half on its side. Bystanders were holding all three of the horses, trying to calm them, a few inspecting the animals to see if they were injured. Two other people were trying desperately to help the driver and the passenger trapped in the wreckage. The driver was propped up and Crowe immediately saw that his arm was at such an impossible angle that it was certainly broken.

Crowe's eyes were drawn to the pale skirts of the

young woman. She was trapped under the weight of the gig, and she was barely moving.

He grasped the arm of the boy who had fetched him. "Help me get to her," he said, knowing that freeing her from the weight of the broken gig was the first thing to do. He saw that one wheel had buckled underneath it, and that the other wheel was broken, and its spokes were sticking out. The girl was pinned under this, white-faced, her eyes wide open. She was biting her lip as if to stop herself from screaming. The scarlet stain around her was already spreading, soaking up her skirt.

Crowe kneeled beside her. "I'm going to stop the bleeding," he said gently. "Then we'll get you out of here. Just for now, keep still."

She tried to nod, but her head barely moved.

He looked at her more carefully. Exactly where did the wheel and its shaft cross her body? What bones were broken? He had seen many accidents on the roadside, others on decks of ships, and on the wharfs. Very seldom were women involved. The women he did see were more often in the clinic, worn out, ill with too much work and too little food. Having child after child had used up all their bodies' resources.

This young woman was different. She was too young to be worn down with anxiety, and she clearly did not

19

lack home, food, or safety. She looked little more than twenty, and her clothes, although now torn and soiled, were of high quality and looked expensive.

Crowe had to tear open her skirt to see exactly what the injuries were, where the main bleeding was coming from, and then stop it—in any way that worked. There was no time to waste. Two or three minutes could be too long.

He worked quickly, cutting away enough of the cloth to reveal the wound. It was bleeding badly, and he suspected that the femoral artery had been nicked. He had to stop any more loss of blood before she bled to death.

He put his hands on the wound and pressed above the torn artery. By the grace of God, it was not a large tear, or she would be dead by now. But he needed help. He looked round. "Anyone here with clean hands?" he called out.

No answer. He must control his frustration. These people were frightened, unsure if they knew how to help. There was a laundry woman a few yards away. "Help me," he called to her. "She'll bleed to death if you don't."

She came forward, her face pale. "I've birthed a few babes, but I never done this sort of thing."

Crowe ripped the cleanest strip of cloth from the

young woman's skirt and placed it over the wound. "Hold this," he said.

The laundry woman looked at her hands doubtfully. They were not clean.

"Never mind the soap, just press here," he insisted, guiding her hands. "I need to repair this tear before she loses any more blood."

The woman looked at him for only a second or two, then focused on the task. Crowe knew that this couldn't be the first serious situation she'd encountered. He shifted one of her hands so it grasped the girl's leg, then he opened his bag.

There was no time to explain what he was going to do. The girl's eyes were looking desperate, a little glassy. Perhaps she understood just how frail a grip she had on life. She could see the blood. How could she not be frightened?

Crowe removed the cloth. He had to find the exact point of the tear and close it. If not, the blood could not circulate and the leg could become gangrenous. If this happened, she was unlikely to live. Or, at the least, she could lose her leg. He glanced into her eyes and smiled briefly. Then he bent to work suturing the wound.

It was a painstaking task, and he had to move quickly. He looked up and saw that the girl was barely breathing. There was no point in saving her leg and losing her life!

The woman assisting him moved hesitantly to mop up the blood so he could see what he was doing. She, too, used part of the girl's dress. Crowe thought for a moment that it was a shame it had been ruined, but it was the best they had.

Finally, he was able to close the artery. With the last suture in place, he leaned back on his haunches and waited. One second, two . . . five. Yes, the sutures were going to hold!

He turned his attention to the secondary wound, the one around the artery. He was about to tell the laundress how grateful he was, but she was focusing on tearing off more of the dress and speaking to the girl.

"It's all right, love, yer doing fine," she said gently.

Crowe glanced at the girl, saw a hint of light in her eyes, and thought how dreadful her pain must be. He bent to work again.

Time seemed to drag by, but each minute brought Crowe closer to treating all of her wound. The young woman was still ashen and her eyes were barely focused. He had a little brandy in his case, just a small bottle. He took it out and held it to her lips.

She did not move.

Was he too slow? Too late? His breath almost choked him. Had she endured all this horror and pain for nothing?

He pressed a few drops of brandy into her mouth, just enough for her to taste, but she seemed unable to swallow.

Seconds went by. Her throat finally moved, and then she was swallowing.

"Come on," he said hoarsely. "Just one more." He put a few more drops between her lips. And then another few, about a teaspoonful this time.

Her eyelids fluttered. She drew in a deep breath. Seconds ticked by, until she opened her eyes and stared at him.

"You're going to be all right," he said very softly. "It'll hurt, but that will pass. You'll get stronger. It's beginning to heal already." That was a bit of an exaggeration, but it felt good to say it, and he could see that she was trying hard to believe him.

Crowe looked around at the gathered crowd. They were watching, fascinated and appalled, willing her to live. He saw that the driver of the large dray, who was being supported by people on either side and was apparently fully conscious, was among those watching.

One man came forward. "We can get a sort of plank.

23

With two men carrying her on it, we can take her wherever you say. The driver can follow."

"Thank you," said Crowe. "My clinic is not far away. I can keep watch on her, make sure nothing starts to bleed again, and treat him. I've got all the medicines." But he knew that more than medicine would be needed, if they were going to keep her alive and safe for the time it would take for the shock to wear off. And he would have to re-dress the wound with clean linen, and make sure there was no infection. And, above all, no gangrene. Please God, there was not! If there was, he would have no other way to save her life than to remove the whole leg. He would have to watch her every moment. "Yes, a plank will do," he said.

"Right you are," the man said, then turned to his friends.

Within minutes, the plank was ready, with two men standing by to help Crowe lift his patient onto it. The driver trailed close behind with a pair of men supporting him.

The young woman was carried safely the short distance to the clinic. As soon as Crowe entered, he rushed to one of the empty beds and helped the two men transfer her onto it.

Once he checked her bandages, she drifted off, and

he worked on the gig's driver, setting his arm and checking that he wasn't in shock. As soon as this was done, he asked about the identity of the young woman.

"That's Miss Hollister," the driver said. "Daughter of Albert Hollister."

"We need to contact him at once," said Crowe. He saw fear cross the man's eyes. "What?"

"Mr. Hollister watches his daughter very carefully," the driver explained. "If he blames me for this accident, I'll never work again."

Crowe thought about this for a moment. "Everyone at the scene said it wasn't your fault, so I'll be sure to tell him that."

The man's expression shifted to relief and then gratitude.

"But we have to let him know . . . now," Crowe added.

The man stood, protecting his broken arm, and walked to the door. Outside, several people were milling about. He spoke quietly to one of the men, who rushed off.

Thirty minutes later, Crowe was standing at the girl's bedside, and her father was bending over her.

"She has a serious wound," Crowe said.

"Serious . . . how serious?" her father asked, his face anxious and annoyed at his own helplessness.

"A tear in the femoral artery, luckily not too large. I was able to suture it closed," Crowe replied.

The man stared at the scarecrow-like doctor, surrounded by the signs of poverty. "And if you had failed?"

Crowe didn't answer. The girl was watching him, eyes open now, and he didn't want her to be afraid.

"Well?" Hollister demanded more loudly.

Crowe took a deep breath. He was a doctor, and he was expected to be truthful. "She might not have survived."

The man thought about this for a moment. "Well, thank you. Now I'll take her home. Our personal physician can come to the house and examine her injury, in case improvements need to be made in the treatment."

Crowe wanted more than anything to protect her, and also convince this man of his skills, but he knew better than to oppose him. There was no bond stronger than that between a parent and child. Still, he could not help but share his professional opinion. "I'm sorry, Mr. Hollister, but she shouldn't be moved."

"Nonsense," Hollister declared. "What could possibly happen?"

"Well, for one thing, the sutures could be compromised and she could start to bleed again. I just checked them when we arrived here. Also," Crowe added, not comfortable with having to frighten this man into complying, "the short trip could expose her to infection, which could lead to gangrene."

"Gangrene?" the man repeated, the color draining from his face.

"I'm afraid so."

"Papa," the girl spoke for the first time, her voice weak but insistent. "Let me stay here, please. Just another day or two, and then I can come home." She looked at Crowe. "Could our family doctor come here to see me?"

"Yes, of course," said Crowe. "An excellent idea."

It was decided that she would stay, and that her physician would come as soon as possible. Her father did nothing to hide the disdain he felt about leaving his daughter in such shoddy surroundings.

Several hours later, the doctor arrived. He looked around the clinic, a far cry from his pristine and expensively stocked rooms, and seemed troubled. However, after examining Ellie's wound, and paying particular attention to the manner of sutures and sterilization, he turned to her father. "The place may not be to our standards, Albert, but this young man knows what he's doing. And I agree: it would increase Ellie's risk to move her."

27

*E*ven after the passage of time, Crowe could still recall that long night, and the longer day following it. He had not left Ellie's side, except to fetch water and a little light broth and, when she was ready, a small serving of soup. The expression on her face told him she didn't like it, but she ate.

To keep her mind away from her fear and discomfort, he talked to her about all sorts of things, especially that first night, when she was in too much pain to sleep. She did not answer him, but he knew from her eyes that she heard his tales of rounding Cape Horn in the Southern Ocean in a three-masted schooner. He described the beauty and terror of it: the huge rock face rearing its head out of the sea, and the worst storms on earth.

He changed the bandages, each time checking that the wound was not bleeding and that it was beginning to show red, healthy flesh, a sign that blood was flowing normally to the area around the wound, and down her leg. He knew that disturbing the dressing at all was bound to hurt her, but she did her best to hide it.

"I'm sorry," he said each time, bitterly regretting what he had to do.

She smiled at him, although it was clear that she hurt too much to speak.

"It's looking good," he said gently. "No gangrene. That's what matters. It's hurting because it's alive."

She lay still, not speaking, just breathing in and out slowly, trying to hang on to her composure. He would have given anything to take the pain for her, but of course it was not possible. All he could do was talk to her, be silent when she needed to concentrate on battling the pain, then sit quietly when she lapsed into sleep.

The following day, she began to speak, and they talked of all kinds of things of heartfelt importance, and also some that were trivial and funny, surprising them into laughter. She wanted to talk. Her mother had been dead for some time, and most of her connections were formal, always watched, always overheard. Being in the clinic was far outside of her privileged but restricted life, and she felt the freedom to be honest.

Her father came a few times to visit. Crowe thought it was more to assure himself that his daughter was being properly cared for. Nevertheless, Albert Hollister was more agreeable now. He even told Crowe to send him the bill when she returned home.

Thinking back to that time, Crowe wasn't sure why

he had never done that. The clinic certainly needed the money!

*W*hen Ellie finally went home, she was recovering well and walking with two crutches.

Crowe had felt an intense gratitude for her healing, and at the same time a hollow ache of loneliness that he knew no one else could fill, once she was gone. He visited her at home on two occasions, explaining to her father that he needed to check on her progress. A few days after the second visit, Albert Hollister sent a messenger with a small donation to the clinic. Crowe responded with a note of thanks, and the offer to come again to check on Ellie. Her father never replied.

*N*ow, all this time later, here was Crowe standing near Ellie's house. What would he say if she saw him? That he wanted to be sure she was fully recovered? Ridiculous! No, it was better to say that he was returning to the clinic after checking on a patient who lived nearby.

The image of Ellie Hollister now took over his mind. He had not spoken to her since his last visit to her home, which had been supervised by the staff. She was not part of his world. She had been, during those terrifying, pain-filled days, but they were fleeting, here and then gone again.

Perhaps that was all she felt: that the time had come and gone. She had treated him as a doctor, as did scores of people. But to him she had been far more than a patient. He wanted desperately to go to her door, ask to speak to her, but that would be considered inappropriate. Perhaps it was better to leave the situation as it was, and not break the magic of memory.

And if she saw him, would she think of him only as it related to pain?

Crowe picked up his pace and followed the street to the long road beside the river, and then entered his clinic. He was glad to see that Scuff was busy. At the moment, he did not want to talk to anyone.

*T*wo days later, in the afternoon, when the sun was only just beginning to slope a little down the sky, and the ships at anchor were gently swinging the other way on their ropes, now facing upstream as the water pulled them east, toward the distant sea, Crowe was walking along the same street, Ellie's Street.

He had collected two bottles of good-quality claret, which he used sparingly. Whenever he had patients with serious wounds, or recovering from illnesses of a gravity that had taken them too close to death, a few sips of this often helped.

He nearly turned round when he saw Ellie standing on the street corner under the lamp, not yet lit. She looked exactly as he remembered her, only she was not favoring one leg. Nevertheless, her body was tense. She was facing the young man who stood opposite her, and a little too close for good manners. She was leaning away from him, but she did not move, even though he was obviously speaking to her, and from the expression on his face, angrily.

She tipped her head a little further back and looked up at him. He was not tall, of just average height, and he was solidly built. Ellie was slender, and Crowe knew that she could easily be knocked off balance. The wound, although healed, had robbed her leg of its original strength. He knew that the draining of that power meant that one leg might always be weaker than the other.

Crowe was too far away to hear, but he could see her lips move. She seemed to be arguing with the man, staring straight into his face and shaking her head.

"You will do as you're told!" he shouted, raising his voice to be loud enough for Crowe to hear from across the street.

A few yards away, coming down the footpath and close enough to hear them, a middle-aged man shook his head. Crowe was watching for him to intervene, but instead he merely touched his hat in a salute, more to the young man than to Ellie. "Evening, Mr. Dolan," he said briefly. "Miss . . ." He left it unfinished, not as if he did not know her name, but as if it did not matter.

Dolan! Crowe knew the name. This must be Paul Dolan, the son of Silas Dolan, a very wealthy man. He owned or had a financial interest in many businesses that imported luxury goods. It was rumored that the senior Dolan held part interest in more than one ship. Crowe did not know the man, but he had heard that this was not a good person to cross. People tended to give him a wide berth and do whatever he wanted. But what was his son, Paul, doing with Ellie? And why was he treating her with such disrespect?

The ugliest answer leaped to Crowe's mind first,

because it was the one he most feared. Ellie's father, Albert Hollister, was in the warehousing business. His path had to have crossed that of Silas Dolan. One had goods, the other the place to store them. Were they partners? Had the two fathers arranged for their children to marry? They couldn't be rivals or enemies, not if their children were betrothed.

The thought made his stomach turn. These alliances were made often, as a way of creating a powerful business partnership. Was this the case? How else to explain this joining of Ellie and Paul, the sweet with the bitter, and the tone he had taken with her?

Crowe suddenly realized that Paul had taken Ellie by the wrist, and from the pain in her face it was clear that he was holding her too hard.

"You will learn to do as you're told, Ellie," he said between his teeth, and yet again loud enough for Crowe to hear. "And without giving me an argument every time. Didn't your father teach you any obedience? Why must you argue with me?"

"Don't shout at me!" she said, trying to free her wrist from his grasp.

Crowe strained to hear the words.

"I'll do as I want!" Paul said back at her.

Crowe felt his muscles tense and his fists clench.

34

The street was bare of traffic for a few moments and unusually quiet, but at this time of day, that would soon change.

Ellie snatched her hand away.

Paul Dolan slapped her. Not hard, but it was across the side of her face.

Crowe glanced up and down the street, then strode across and, within seconds, was at the opposite side. He grabbed Paul's arm and twisted it sharply behind the man's back. He heard a crack, a gasp of pain, and then the man's shoulder went limp.

Paul tried to swing back, his face twisted with fury, but the best he could do was lunge at Crowe, who moved sideways. Dolan's weight behind that lunge carried him forward, causing him to stumble over his own feet. And then, overbalancing on the curb, he fell hard into the gutter.

Crowe did nothing to stop his fall.

There was a second of silence in which no one moved.

Ellie turned to Crowe, her eyes wide, and then she looked beyond him to Paul Dolan, who was slowly climbing to his feet, clumsily, as if he was not sure his legs would hold his weight, and grasping his shoulder where Crowe had wrenched it.

Crowe looked away from Ellie. He had to watch

Dolan. If this man would strike a woman, then he would not be above pummeling a man from behind.

Dolan swayed a moment longer and then steadied himself. He glared at Ellie, then at Crowe. "Who the hell are you?" he demanded. "How dare you interfere in my family affairs? If I tell my wife to do something, that is my right! If you interfere again, I'll teach you your place! Whoever you are, I'll ruin you. Do you hear me?"

Crowe froze. Ellie was his wife?

"I am not your wife," she said, almost choking on her words.

Dolan glared at her. "Not yet! But we'll be married soon enough. Get Christmas over, and then the wedding."

"I don't want . . ." She shook her head, but she did not finish the sentence.

"You love your father?" Dolan asked. He was stained with mud from the gutter and there was a bruise darkening on his skin from the fall. He was still an impressive figure, even while clutching his shoulder awkwardly. He was very muscular beneath his carefully cut suit and coat, a man who could do serious harm if provoked. His thick dark hair was cut skillfully. Only his expression let him down.

Ellie wilted. "Of course I do," she said quietly.

"Then you will do as he wishes," Paul said with a tight-lipped smile. "You have the power to help him return to the prosperity he once had . . . and to keep him there." And then he added, "Or not."

Ellie started to say something, and then changed her mind. She looked beaten. Her eyes lowered and she seemed to be avoiding Crowe's look.

"Thank you," she said very quietly. Her words were clearly for Crowe, although she did not meet his eyes. "It was a misunderstanding. My fiancé did not mean to hurt me. He . . . he would not do that."

It was very clearly a lie, but Crowe sensed that she was compelled to say it. He was in no position to interfere, although everything in him screamed against that decision.

He searched for something to say, and then found it. "He needs to go to his doctor and have his shoulder treated."

Paul Dolan glared at him, then blinked, still holding his upper arm. "You'll come with me!" he told Ellie.

She shook her head. "No, I'll go home." She glanced in the direction of her house, which was within view.

"If I leave her here, and if anything happens to her . . ." Paul began.

Ellie turned toward him. "Nothing will happen to me, Paul. Please, look after yourself."

He glared at Crowe for a long moment, then turned on his heel and limped away.

Crowe wanted to say something, but nothing sensible came to his tongue. He was standing alone with her, his mind filled with intense emotion, and he could find no words.

After a moment, she asked, "Were you here to visit me?"

"I have a patient who lives a few streets away," he said. "That is, he's the gardener."

She nodded, her face still reflecting the embarrassment of being seen in this unpleasant domestic dispute.

"I will see you safely home," Crowe promised.

"If you are busy, Dr. Crowe, I can walk the two minutes it will take to get to my door. I promise, I should be quite safe," she said.

"Nonsense. I insist," he replied.

In the fading light, he saw the faint color rise in her cheeks, but he wasn't sure that what flashed across her face was a shy smile.

Ellie turned away and began to walk along the pavement, slightly uphill.

It took him three strides to catch up with her. He

wanted to find something to say to her in these few precious minutes, but nothing seemed appropriate. He did not want to fill this silence with platitudes, but what could he say that would mean anything at all?

It was she who broke the silence between them. "How is your clinic doing? I hear good things about it, but it is all secondhand, from people who know someone who has been helped."

"There are good days and bad," Crowe replied. "But we always find enough to survive. Sometimes it comes from the most surprising people. It's pennies, but more often it's food, a fresh loaf of bread, some eggs, an apple pie." He smiled at the memory of the shy offerings of homemade goods, such as soft cloths that would do for bandages, and an extra nightshirt for someone who did not have one. "Even a bag of tea leaves." He had learned early on that strong tea was a lifter of spirits, a reviver of energy.

He looked at her, and saw her quickly blinking away her gathering tears, and perhaps memories of the gifts she had seen when she was there, gifts from people who had so little.

For a moment, they stood in silence. Before he had spoken, it seemed as if Ellie had several things to say, but then this mention of his gratitude for having received gifts from those who had so little seemed to have awakened in her emotions that were taking several moments to control.

The hill was quite steep in front of her home and they leaned forward a little into the climb. There was much to say, but everything that mattered, he should not say. Not only was it unwise, and far too self-revealing, but they were things she would not want to know, that might prove embarrassing and totally futile. He should, at the least, leave himself a bit of dignity!

Again, it was she who broke the silence. "How is Scuff doing?" While Crowe had treated Ellie and sat by her bedside, he told her of his mentee, and she had been charmed by stories of their collaboration. She met Scuff only briefly during her stay, but she felt as though she knew him.

Her question was safe, and easy to answer. "Well," he said. "In fact, he's doing very well. He has the skills to be a fine doctor, and he's gaining new knowledge every day. He remembers everything. I suppose that comes from so many years of not being able to read and having to rely on his memory, and also from having to do calculations in his head." He smiled. "And then, when Hester Monk taught him how to read and write, I'm guessing that there was no holding him back. I think he still sees a sort of magic in words. The way squiggly marks on a page can lead us to capture ideas, facts, emotions. Whether they're on a piece of paper, a clay tablet, or anything else that can hold an image. Of course, we can draw pictures of solid things, but not ideas. Only words can do that. For Scuff, it's still a kind of enchantment, a thing of the spirit."

She smiled at him. "It's a pity we ever lose that, isn't it? It's like standing in the sun for so long you become comfortable, and then forget what it was like to be cold."

They came to the curb. He wished to take her arm, then realized it might be seen as an imposition. She was not infirm. He had no right to do this, so he let his hand fall and walked beside her.

Once they were on the lengthy footpath leading to her door, he started to tell her about some of the cases he had treated. She had spent enough time in bed at the clinic, too ill to be moved, to know very well that not all cases could be helped. There were always some patients for whom the only thing Crowe could do was to ease their pain, or make someone's death as free from agony or fear as possible.

It seemed to Crowe that both he and Ellie were happy to let that remain mutually understood.

When they reached her door, they were surrounded

by the house's elegant façade, the trees in the front garden, the evergreen holly bushes gleaming with red berries, and the streetlamps right beside the gate. Crowe hesitated.

"I'll go in the back door," she said quietly. "And I will tell Papa only as much as I have to."

He understood. She might be protecting herself against her father's anger. If she told him about Paul Dolan's behavior, would he believe her? Perhaps he could not afford to, if he needed Silas Dolan on his side. After all, the senior Dolan had the reputation of a powerful man who was quick to anger. It occurred to Crowe that his son came by his arrogance through family tradition, example, even inheritance.

"I'll see you inside," he answered.

She paused for a moment, as if trying to decide the wisdom of this.

$C$rowe knew that the easiest thing would be to leave her as soon as the door had been opened by a servant, but he wanted to see Albert Hollister. Would it be a challenge to his own temper to speak civilly to the man?

And what if he mentioned Paul's behavior? Hollister might well accuse him of meddling, or inappropriate behavior, which would only make it harder for Ellie.

The back door opened and a man stood there. Crowe assumed he was waiting for Ellie. From his black jacket and pressed trousers, it was clear that he was the butler.

Ellie was ready for him. "Good evening, Barker. I'm afraid Mr. Dolan slipped and fell in the street. He was quite wet." Her voice quivered a little.

Crowe thought she was suppressing laughter. He hoped it was that and not tears. Or worse, a dread of what her father might say.

"Dr. Crowe was passing, and he insisted on walking me home," she finished.

"Thank you, Doctor," Barker said gravely, then turned back to Ellie. "I hope Mr. Dolan was not injured, miss." It was not really a question, more a polite thing to say, closing the matter.

"No, nothing serious, Barker. Is Papa at home? Perhaps you could tell him I am safely in?"

She wanted to avoid her father. Crowe could hear it in her voice, and apparently the butler could also.

"Yes, miss," he said gravely, and turned toward the inner door leading into the back kitchen.

At that moment, the door swung open and Albert Hollister stood there, effectively blocking the way.

Crowe surmised that he had been slender in his youth. He was not heavily boned, and at least three inches shorter than Crowe. The man was portly now, and his silver hair less abundant than it had been even last spring. His face darkened when he saw Crowe. It was clear that he recognized him immediately, which was not surprising. Not only was Crowe tall, but he always dressed in black. Often it was a long-tailed jacket, as now, sometimes an open overcoat, or even oilskins in the worst weather. His face was strong, keen, and his wild hair a dense black. Despite this, his voice was soft and clear, as though he were a gentleman fallen on hard times. He never explained to anyone where he had got his diction, or his vocabulary.

"What the devil are you doing here?" Hollister demanded. "Do you require more money?" He said it with an intonation that gave it the weight of an insult.

Ellie closed her eyes and seemed to shrink into herself. Even Barker blanched.

Crowe breathed in, and then out. He must not make this worse! "If you wish to give money to the clinic, sir, so that more of the poor may be treated, then do so directly to the clinic. I believe you know where it is."

44

It was the butler who intervened. "Mr. Dolan has had an accident, sir, and was not able to continue with Miss Eliza. Dr. Crowe merely came the last distance to be sure she arrived safely."

"How do you know that?" Hollister demanded. "Did he say so?"

"No, sir, Miss Eliza did," the butler replied. He was an extremely well-trained servant. He understood how to behave as a gentleman and had clearly done so for far longer than his master. Crowe wondered if Hollister was aware of that.

Hollister stared at Crowe, who met his gaze and stared back. Only Ellie glanced at the butler with warmth.

"I'm obliged," Hollister said stiffly to Crowe. "I thought I made it plain when my daughter left your clinic that once she was healed, that was to be the end of your acquaintance." His eyebrows rose. "What part of that arrangement did you not understand?"

"As Mr. Barker explained, sir, I merely accompanied Miss Hollister because she is a young lady whose escort fell into the gutter." Crowe kept his expression absolutely blank, as if he did not see the double meaning to his words. "He needed to change his clothes, since he was wet and covered with dirt. I require no thanks from you for having accompanied Miss Hollister to her home. Any decent man would have done as much. I think you should know that Mr. Dolan was violent, sir. Perhaps you are unaware of it, or you would have put a stop to it by now. I fear that your daughter might be too afraid of him to tell you that herself."

Hollister's face flushed red. "I'll thank you to mind your own business, mister . . . Doctor. We are obliged to you for your help when my daughter had an accident, but we have paid you for your services, and that is the end of the matter, Doctor . . . whatever—I'm sorry, I forget your surname—thank you for walking home with my daughter. Tell me, what do I owe you for that service?" He must have seen Crowe's face, because he stopped.

Ellie gasped, then almost choked on her words, forcing them out. "Papa, Dr. Crowe does not want paying, as if he were your servant." She turned to Crowe, but she could not look him in the eye. "I'm sorry. I would not have let you see me safely home if I'd known you would be insulted. Please forgive my clumsiness."

Crowe drew a deep breath. "No apology is needed, Miss Hollister. I can see your father did not mean to be as rude as he sounded. He is only anxious for your safety . . . and your welfare."

46

He turned to Albert Hollister and did not even pretend to smile. "Your manners reflect your concern. There is no need to explain the depth of your feelings. Nevertheless, Mr. Dolan seems a very ill-controlled young man. Good evening to you, sir." And with a brief glance at the butler, and avoiding Ellie's eyes, he turned and walked to the back door, opened it, and went out into the now-dark early evening.

Crowe walked toward the clinic. Since he had run into Ellie and Paul, the lamplighter had passed along these roads, well above the streets and alleys of the dockside, and had lit all the lamps, allowing Crowe to see the pavement.

Lower down, near the water and all its multitudinous trades and businesses, and carrying far heavier traffic, few of the streets had pavements at all, and those that had were paved unevenly, worn by the endless passage of feet. Nevertheless, he was able to walk almost by instinct, feeling his way along the cracks and, above all, avoiding tripping. After so many years living in this area, he knew the potholes and uneven levels as well as if he could see them.

He walked into the dark night and realized that his mind was made up. He could not leave it alone and just walk away. He must find out all he could about Albert

Hollister . . . and Paul Dolan as well. Marrying this Dolan fellow was clearly not what Ellie wanted, and yet she was willing to accept it . . . or so she insisted. Why? There must be a reason. It was none of Crowe's business, and yet he could not stand apart. Paul Dolan was in every way objectionable. He was crude, a bully, even violent at the least provocation. Why would any man wish his daughter to marry such a person? Was there some hidden goodness in the young man that Crowe could not see, and Ellie could? He knew many awkward, unpolished people. In fact, most of his patients were without money, education, or any social graces, except those bestowed on them by good nature. But they were not violent.

No, there was something more urgent here, and more tangible. He must find out. First, he would learn more about Albert Hollister, then about Paul Dolan, and Silas, his father.

In the little time they had spent together, he had learned all kinds of things about Ellie's character, her hopes and dreams. He'd discovered what made her laugh and what disgusted her. He had discovered what stirred her to anger and to grief. But he knew very few actual facts about her life, except the medical ones he learned as a result of her accident. She had told him her mother had died some years ago of an illness, nothing mysterious or springing from any fault in her care. He had also learned that Ellie was an only child.

There was an ocean of things he did not know. If he acted without at least some knowledge, he could do far more harm than good.

But if he did not help her, who would?

He made a list in his mind of things he needed to do. His memory was extraordinary, and he seldom wrote anything down, except for medical orders. That was a characteristic he shared with Scuff. The benefactor who had helped Crowe learn to read and write was a ship's surgeon, who had taught him anatomy and medicine during their long days at sea. Then came university, and a learning he had absorbed with a passion, much as the driest sponge absorbs water. Much as Scuff was doing now.

Then had come the scandal, disaster, that had ruined his benefactor and cut off the finances that had paid his fees. It was the end of his formal studies. But he never abandoned medicine: it was his art, his calling, and his love. He had wandered about for a while, worked with animals, which he had loved, then returned to London and was drawn into helping people. He knew it was illegal. He had the knowledge, but not the official title

49

that comes with passing examinations that made it legal to practice medicine.

It was Hester Monk, who would later become Scuff's adoptive mother, who had persuaded Crowe to return to his formal studies and earn his qualifications. She knew far more about practical medical care than many doctors. It came from participating in surgeries on the battlefields in the Crimea. It was from her that Scuff, too, acquired his love of healing, and his ambition to give his life over to it.

Crowe had not taken Scuff in as a favor to Hester. It was for Scuff's own sake, but it was also because Crowe saw an echo of his younger self in the boy. The boy who was now a man.

Crowe was determined to learn what he could about Albert Hollister and the Dolan family. Discovering more about what their businesses were would be simple enough, but he needed to understand what anchored those businesses . . . the facts that could not be readily seen. For example, who owned them? Did Silas Dolan trade alone, or did he have partners? And to whom did he and Hollister owe money, loyalty, or repayment of favors? Sometimes, the very nature of debt could run deep, and it could be dangerous. At the same time, he wanted to know if someone—Hollister?—had a debt to Dolan. Crowe wondered what he might discover.

His mind returned to the subject of families and, specifically, businesses. Was it possible that one of the businesses, headed by either Dolan or Hollister, was failing? And if that happened, who would lose? What secrets tied the Dolan and Hollister families together?

Perhaps, Crowe decided, he should first learn about Hollister, what he owed, if anything, and to whom. And then the same about Silas Dolan.

Crowe was convinced that there was a nefarious link between the two men, one that added up to Ellie being promised in marriage to a brutish young man.

He knew who to ask, and he would start tomorrow.

The wind blew up from the river, sharp and cold on the incoming tide. He put his head down as he went round a corner. Only half a mile to go and he would be home.

The shops he passed reminded him that Christmas was only a little over a week away, but he felt none of the joy of the festive season.

*C*rowe had more contacts among ordinary people than anyone he knew. There were the regular police and the Thames River Police, firemen, and the ferrymen who rode back and forth across the river. There were dock-side workers, cab drivers, news vendors—both of news-papers and posters—and peddlers of everything from matches and bootlaces to fresh ham sandwiches. The newspaper vendors always knew more than the papers they sold, and then there were the running patterers. These were the men who heard pieces of news mixed with gossip and exaggeration, to which they added a little music and lots of rhyming slang, and entertained the public on the street. They were the main source of news for the masses that could not read. Crowe knew a few of them. He liked their sly wit, their crazy rhymes and rhythms. Sometimes, they were informed about more than they thought it was wise to say, but with a little skill and good humor, they could be persuaded to reveal what they knew. These men were natural racon-teurs, street poets, and actors.

By the time Crowe reached the clinic and was inside, sheltered, and warm, it was late. He was tired and hun-gry, but his mind was racing.

Scuff was in the kitchen stirring the big saucepan that lived on the back of the stove. It contained lots of bones, fresh ones added every two or three days, plus cabbage stalks and potato peelings. Always onions, and sometimes barley, very often turnips.

He breathed in deeply. He had not even thought of it, but now he realized that he hadn't eaten for a long time, too consumed had he been with his thoughts.

Scuff heard him and turned around. "Hungry?" he asked.

For the first time since seeing Ellie Hollister on the street, Crowe smiled. He felt the stiffness ease out of his body. "Yes, I am," he said. "Any new patients?" He sat down at the kitchen table.

"Nothing much," Scuff replied, turning back to the saucepan. "A couple of cuts that needed a stitch, couple of bad colds. Gave them some of that vile cough medicine." He shot a grin at Crowe. "Tastes so vile it'll be some time before they finish it! You think it really works? If it does, I'll make some more."

Crowe smiled. "Yes, do make more. It keeps. By the way, unless there's a rash of accidents, or something serious, I'll be out most of the time over the next day or so. I'm looking into something."

"Can I help?" Scuff asked, a hint of excitement in his voice.

"Yes," said Crowe. "You can be here and look after things. Please?" When he saw how Scuff nodded as he realized with anticipation that he would be left in charge of the clinic, Crowe felt relieved. The clinic would be in good hands. He could leave with an easy mind, and put his whole attention into learning about Silas Dolan and Albert Hollister.

*W*hen Crowe set out early the following morning, he was quite certain where he would begin. He was also quite certain that he did not want to know the full truth about Albert Hollister, because he was afraid of what it would tell him about Ellie. As much as he knew he should, he could not get her out of his thoughts. He never would. She had been moved to the back of his mind and had remained there most of the time, a sweet and distant memory, but being with her after this short space of time had shattered his delicate self-deception.

Ellie was real again, with no protection of dreams, and desperately vulnerable. Not that she had asked for his help. In fact, when she had walked away from Paul Dolan, she seemed to have had only a momentary relief, and it was quite clear in her eyes, in the whole set of her face, that she intended to continue her course with him.

Bitter as this was for Crowe, it was clearly her choice.

But now Crowe was on a quest. He needed to know

why. What did he expect to find? Something that would offer her an escape? No, he was looking for the truth, the reason why she did not walk away from Paul Dolan and his repellent behavior. The thought of him hurting her made him feel ill. Dolan's slapping her, and even touching her intimately—the very idea felt like blasphemy. Crowe could still see the look in her eyes, the pain in them. And when she had turned away from him, he knew that she recognized Dolan's cruelty and could do nothing.

But why?

What did Crowe not understand? Whatever it was, he felt compelled to discover the reason behind it. Seeing her again had awakened within him all those feelings of tenderness, the intimacy of not being alone in the heart, the happiness of sharing as he never had with anyone as far back as his memory stretched, including the darker years of his childhood.

The time Ellie had spent in the clinic, recovering from what could have been a fatal injury, had made him aware of loneliness, a kind of separation from something infinitely precious, but only half remembered. Her presence had released all of this. In that short stay, he had learned to trust her always to be herself, good and yet fallible; frightened but never a coward; tender, wanting to trust, even for the short time she had been there, before returning to the shadows of her life and to her inescapable duties. He would not have wanted her to be different, whatever her hungers or her fears, or to be taken away from what was her duty.

But was this relationship with Paul Dolan really her duty, regardless of what it cost her? When Crowe had treated her, Dolan had not been part of the picture. Or had he? Was he always there, and it was only that Crowe had not known it? That was another truth he did not want to face, and yet he must.

Exactly where should he begin, if he wanted to learn about Albert Hollister? There were a few things that Ellie had told him about her father. He knew, of course, that Hollister was a widower and Ellie was his only child. And that, financially, he was very comfortable. She had not actually said that, but it emerged through their conversations. And he could see this for himself, from the quality of her clothes, ruined as they were in the accident. Nevertheless, he knew the feel of quality, of fine cotton lawn, rather than the coarse cotton he was accustomed to seeing. And when her father had come to take her home, she had changed into clothing that was clearly of high quality.

What else had she told him in those few days together? He had encouraged her to talk while in terrible pain, mostly to take her mind off it, if even for a moment. And . . . because he was interested.

So, what did he know? Albert Hollister owned warehouses, several of them along the waterfront of the south bank of the Thames. Merchants needed them when loading and unloading, storing goods of all kinds that would be carried by rail to elsewhere, or sold to merchants here in London. It was a good business, and he had prospered from it.

But that was information Crowe had learned nearly a year ago, when he was tending to Ellie in the clinic. Had anything changed since then? And did it explain her betrothal to a man she quite clearly despised? Even more than that, a man she feared.

Crowe turned his thoughts to Silas Dolan. How did he fit into Ellie's life, beyond being the father of the bully who was betrothed to her? She had never mentioned the name Dolan during her recovery. Young Dolan had certainly never visited her, unlike her father, who had come to see her on several occasions. Each time, he had tried to take her home, but the sight of his daughter's pale face, recognizing that she was still in pain, and Crowe's warnings about the dangers of moving her, had made him back down. He had put his daughter's safety before his strong opinions, which told Crowe that he cared. So, what had changed so radically since then? Why would he allow someone like Paul Dolan to marry her?

Dolan had spoken to her of their marriage returning her father to the prosperity he had once had. That implied a change in circumstances . . .

If Crowe was going to save Ellie from this terrible fate, he needed answers!

Of all the different kinds of people on the street— people he had treated and assisted, or even those he hardly knew—who could help him now? He hated asking, lest some might see this as a kind of request for repayment. He did what he could to help anyone, but it was always the poor and the desperate who came to him. That was because they knew him, and trusted him, and it had made no difference if they lacked the money to pay a regular doctor. They had trusted him even before Hester Monk had persuaded him to finish his formal education and take the necessary examinations to qualify. If he asked for their help, would they feel obligated, based on his past treatment of them?

Crowe thought of those earlier times. He had never been so afraid of anything in his life as he feared failing to pass the exams. He was terrified that he would be forbidden to practice medicine any longer, having already practiced without qualifications. And what about all the people who had trusted him? He would have to abandon his treatment of them. But when it had come time to take the examinations, he had succeeded! Now he was treating the same people as before, only from a newer and bigger clinic, one with a few rooms where several patients could stay and recover, if the cases were severe enough. He owed Hester Monk for that.

Scuff had more than earned his way in the practice. And any knowledge or confidence Crowe had given him, and would continue to give him, was the cause of profound satisfaction for both of them. No, not just both, but all of them. He had to include Hester and Monk.

Should he ask for Monk's help in this? As the senior policeman on the river, he would have access to all kinds of information about Silas Dolan and his son, Paul, and Albert Hollister as well.

No, before turning to Monk, he first must find out the basic facts that were common knowledge on the street. And it was better if he did so quietly, putting the pieces together until he had enough to form at least a rough picture. He was not researching the way to treat an illness or injury; this was about Ellie Hollister's life!

He began with a man he had helped several years

earlier. Actually, he had saved him from losing his hand after a river injury. Several small bones had been crushed, and it was Crowe's immediacy on the scene and his quick responses that had made the difference. This man, Joe, was still making his living on the river, skillfully managing the long strings of barges that went higher up from the Pool of London, with enormous loads of goods for distribution, traveling as far inland as the river stretched, until it was no more than a stream with a very shallow draft. An entire line of these barges could be managed by a single man standing at the stern, using his long pole, his balance, and his minute knowledge of every ridge and sandbank, his awareness of everything about the tides that had taken him along the river since childhood. Joe had learned them all, and now it was instinctive. And he had the good fortune of having two strong hands to manage the pole. With only one hand, he would not have been able to earn a living. And he had Crowe to thank for this.

"What can I do for you?" Joe asked, when Crowe finally found him sheltering behind a stack of crates and boxes.

There was no time to waste in being unnecessarily evasive or devious. And it was probably pointless anyway, an insult to the man's intelligence.

"What do you know about Albert Hollister?" Crowe asked.

Joe thought for a moment. "Hollister's got these warehouses along the river, south side. Two small ones, and one big one with its own wharf. That's a lot, that is, having your own wharf. Get stuff in and out quick." He gave a lopsided wink. "Before anyone gets too much time to wonder what it is exact, like."

"Is it likely to be of interest to, say, the River Police?"

"More like Customs men," Joe replied. "And they got no friends, exceptin' those that try to buy their favors."

"Is Hollister dealing in stuff that Customs would like to know about?" He had to ask, although he did not want to know.

"Not much." Joe pursed his lips. "Too easy to get caught. You need to know all the right people."

"And who are the right people?"

"You born yesterday, Doc? They mostly take a bit on the side, the Customs men do, and keep their mouths shut. "'Ollister is not in anyone's pocket, far as I know. Unless it's Silas Dolan's."

Crowe felt a knot tighten inside his chest. "Are you saying that Albert Hollister is beholden to Silas Dolan?"

"Don't need to be," Joe replied. "They're both cleverer than that. There were days . . . let's just say Dolan made a whole bag full o' money from a fire. Lost a fortune in silks and stuff, so they say . . . but he came out all right . . . if you get my drift."

"What has that to do with Hollister?" Crowe had to ask, although, yet again, he dreaded the answer.

"The fire was in one of Hollister's warehouses."

Crowe nodded, but he knew that uncertainty was clear in his face.

"So, here's what you do, Doc," Joe explained patiently. "You pretend to be uploading the stuff—you know, into some warehouse—when you're really offloading it. That means putting it somewhere safe, where it won't be seen. Can't get much safer than a string o' barges goin' upriver on the tide. So, your warehouse is empty, or nearly so, and all the goods are safe upstream, and then you set fire to the warehouse and claim the insurance. Oh, no! Lost all me silks and furs! Oldest trick in the book, but you gotta be clever about it. Anybody who could prove you did it . . . and you're theirs for life. Like a sword hanging over your 'ead."

Crowe was working to understand this. "But that means it was Silas Dolan who claimed the loss," he concluded.

"Yeah, but he couldn't get his goods out—that is, before the fire—without 'Ollister helping 'im, and knowing it was safe. An' then claiming that everything in that warehouse was lost when it burned to the ground. Then they both got their bit. "'Ollister gets a new warehouse—I heard he built a nice new one, wi' no rot in it—an' Dolan gets insurance payment for the goods. Mind you, 'e's burned a few cartons of things, to be left as proof. And the rest? Guessing he sold the rest up-river."

So, what was Joe saying? That Dolan and Hollister shared insurance fraud? Was that what was binding them? The fire would be easy enough to check on. Crowe knew men he could ask. "Were there other people to pay off?" Crowe asked, wondering how widespread this crime might have been.

Joe shook his head. "Not as you would ask. Bits an' pieces 'ere and there. Night watchman died in the fire, poor sod! An' what happens when you go around asking, Doc? Nothin' good, mark my words. They be finding bits an' pieces of you all up an' down the river!"

Crowe felt the cold take hold of him, as if he had fallen into a slow-moving eddy in an icy river. It took his breath away. He met Joe's eyes, and saw in them the bitterness and certainty that made the next question unnecessary. It died on his lips. If what Joe said was true, then the night watchman's death was not an acci-

dent, it was murder. He had died during the commis-
sion of a crime. This would explain the debt between
the Dolans and Hollister. Ellie was part of the bargain
they had made, all intended by Hollister to keep his
name clean. And to keep him out of prison.

But the police had done nothing! Crowe had known
William Monk for years, and knew him to be an honor-
able man. Why had he done nothing? The warehouse
had been on the river. Having its own wharf was one of
the primary factors that made it so valuable. And Monk
was head of the Thames River Police!

So, *was* it arson? Or was that just gossip? Such stories were frequent. Enemies, rivals, anyone spreading
lies—so many people hoped to profit, or at least exercise
an old vengeance.

And if this was fraud—and, even worse, murder—
did Crowe want to know? Was that what Ellie feared so
much? Was she marrying Paul Dolan to protect her father's reputation? Might his inquiries only dig up what
she was prepared to spend her life protecting? He could
only guess, but he needed to know what Dolan had on
Ellie's father. If Hollister was in cahoots with Dolan,
and he was found out, then Dolan would be exposed as
well.

The thought was sickening. But now that all of these

possibilities had occurred to him, and there seemed to be substance in them, he could not walk away.

*T*he following day, Crowe got up early. He was too wide awake—too keen to continue his quest to learn everything he could about Albert Hollister and Silas Dolan—to lie in bed any longer.

He ate a boiled egg and several slices of bread with jam, and was drinking his second cup of tea when Scuff stumbled in, still half asleep.

"Morning," Crowe said cheerfully. "Tea's still hot. I'm going out. Don't know when I'll be back."

Crowe took a steadying breath. He was being unfair, leaving like this, but it was something he needed to do. And he was confident that Scuff could handle nearly anything that came to the clinic. "I'll call by at about two this afternoon. If an accident or emergency happens before then, I'll probably hear about it. I'm not going far."

"What is it you're preoccupied with?" Scuff asked, his eyes filled with curiosity, and perhaps a touch of anxiety.

Did Crowe owe Scuff an explanation? A longer look at the young man's face told him that he did. And it was far easier to be honest than try to frame an answer, no matter how vulnerable Crowe was feeling. He was uncertain exactly what he meant to do, and also aware that it was in no way Scuff's burden to know. Nor should he be expected to fill in all the spaces that Crowe was leaving, including the daily duties.

"I saw Ellie Hollister in the street," he said, and immediately saw the sharp concern in Scuff's face. The young man had helped to care for Ellie, enough to know her quite well. "She's betrothed to a fellow who was rough with her. I saw him slap her." Before Scuff could respond, and it was clear he was about to, Crowe rushed on. "I need to find out why she's marrying him. It can't be because she loves him; I saw her fear. So why would her father give her to this brute? What kind of bargain did Hollister make?" He stopped. That was explanation enough. He wanted to guard the privacy of his own emotions, and possibly Ellie's reasons for obeying her father when it was clearly against her own feelings. At the same time, Crowe did not want to reveal it all. And there was too much he did not know yet.

When Scuff said nothing, Crowe filled in the silence. "I need to know the truth before I can do anything more." Having said this, he realized that there was almost certainly nothing he could do about it, especially if Hollister had done something illegal. Would Ellie permit a marriage that appeared to revolt her, in order to save her father from shame, even ruin? Crowe knew the answer before he had finished framing the question in his mind. She might not think of it in those same words, but he believed that, yes, she would.

Scuff did not respond to anything Crowe was saying, at least not with words. Finally, he offered a very neutral, "I see. In that case, I can manage here."

Crowe understood what Scuff was actually saying was that he would do his best. Crowe could not ask for more. "Thank you," he said quietly. He wanted to remind Scuff that his best was, in fact, exceptional, but Scuff was still learning, and his confidence was not yet fully formed. His vulnerability was evident.

If Crowe had anything less urgent to accomplish, or for anyone other than Ellie, he might have relented. But Scuff was twenty-two, old enough to go to sea, or be a soldier who sees death every week, sometimes every day. As young as he was, he had witnessed his share of the violence of slaughter caused by the long-drawn-out ruin of disease. And he was good at what he did.

Crowe gave a little nod and took his coat off the hook

by the door. He pulled it on and went outside, putting his head down as he walked into the wind and the rain. He should have said something more to Scuff, but his voice was choked in his throat and he wasn't sure what words he could have used.

*I*t had been a freezing night. The pavement was slippery with a coating of ice, melted in places, some white, some clear as glass and dangerous to the unwary. Black ice, they called it. People would fall today; Crowe hoped there would be no more than bruises and sprains. He must keep his word and check in at the clinic as promised. Could Scuff set a broken ankle bone? He could almost certainly do it. He had helped Crowe set many, but not alone. Scuff deserved to have Crowe there, advising and guiding.

That meant Crowe needed to be organized and not waste time. He should begin with the obvious first. Joe had been helpful, but Crowe needed some corroboration of what he had learned about the connection between Hollister and Silas Dolan.

Jim Prism, who wrote bills of lading, was one of the

former patients with whom he had become friends. It was time to call on him. If he could not help, then Crowe would seek out other former patients.

Jim Prism's office wasn't far from the clinic, and Crowe was soon facing the man. As always, his spectacles were sliding down his nose.

"Good morning, Mr. Prism," Crowe said, closing the office door.

The man was bald, his body shape what some called roly-poly, and an affable face. The red blotches on his cheeks reminded Crowe of Santa Claus, although he suspected they were caused by high blood pressure.

"Good morning, Doc." Prism looked up from his desk, peering over the top of his glasses.

Crowe thought he actually wore them as a kind of badge of office, a reminder to himself that he had achieved some intellectual status. He had no desire to prolong this; time was running out.

"Do you know Mr. Albert Hollister?" Crowe asked, sitting down on the rickety chair facing a desk littered with papers. "Merchant, here on the south bank?"

"Know of him," Prism replied. "He don't need your help, unless he gone and got burned again." He laughed at what he seemed to think was clever humor. "But the insurance'll pay out. They got to for fires, 'aven't they?"

"Not so far as I know," Crowe replied. "But I heard talk about that fire. Was it bad?"

"He said so," Prism replied. "But *bad* depends on what got burned, don't it?" He put his head a little to one side and looked at Crowe very steadily. "I wouldn't tell no one but you, but I s'pose I owe you, and you didn't ask for nothing when you stitched me up, like. And you didn't ask no questions neither. Him and Silas Dolan reckon as they lost thousands o' quids' worth o' goods in that fire. An' the ware'ouse itself, o' course. That was lost, too."

Crowe stiffened slightly. This was just what Joe had said! "And what did the insurers say?"

"There were goods, right enough. Bales o' fine wool and silk, and stuff like that. An' furs as well. Barely a speck of it left, when they finally got the fire out. But, funny 'ow much yardage there were for sale, 'ere an' there, just a month or two after that, if yer knew where to look for it." The remark was made slyly, as if Crowe could pick up the man's suspicions.

"Maybe some of it wasn't burned—is that what you're saying? That the firemen got a lot of it out safely?"

Prism gave him a sideways look. "Yeah, that's right. Do you stitch a burn, or put a plaster on it, huh?" After a moment, he added, "Don't be daft, Doc. They got it out before they ever lit that fire in the first place!" Prism's face was a picture of disgust.

"But they weren't prosecuted. Are you sure it was arson?"

"Yeah," he said, then quickly added, "And there was a dead man." Before Crowe could respond, he said, "Mind, I never said that!" He looked suddenly anxious.

"Of course not," Crowe agreed. "Whatever you say to me is in confidence." Crowe saw the fear ease out of Prism's face. Why was he afraid? Was he frightened of Hollister? Or, more likely, of Silas Dolan? "Thank you," he added.

Crowe sat quietly, giving the man a moment to decide whether to speak or not.

Prism took a deep breath and let it out slowly. "If they'd been brought to trial—Hollister and Dolan—they'd be 'Er Majesty's guests at the Coldbath Fields, as like as not. And certain, except for Bedlam, there ain't no place worse than that. Wouldn't wish it on my worst enemy! Or maybe on him, but not no one else."

"You sure about that?" Crowe pressed, with a tinge of humor in his voice.

"If you could even ask that, then you never seen the Coldbath Fields. Worst prison in England, that is."

"So I heard," Crowe conceded. "I don't need to see it for myself." He stood. "Thank you, Mr. Prism."

The man smiled broadly. "You're welcome!"

Crowe walked out into the street again, his mind swirling with thoughts. And worse than that, images. Warehouse fires happened every now and again. Only a fool did not insure. A fool, or someone too hard up to afford the insurance. But his imagination was still playing with the fear that this was only the first touch of a dark shadow of violence that was hidden behind the docks, the warehouses, the huge ships lying at anchor in the Pool of London, and the vast city beyond.

Fire was a dreadful weapon, he knew that too well, but it was also a powerful tool, treacherous to the changes of wind by even one point of the compass. It was something he had only seen the edges of, in the few victims who had survived, and in the stories firemen only hinted at. He had seen burned bodies. He had never been closer than a hundred yards to a fire, and he could still recall the feeling of waves of heat burning his hair.

Was Albert Hollister in debt to Silas Dolan over this warehouse fraud? And even more, the death of someone? Was that why Ellie would accept marrying Paul Dolan? Crowe could not blame her for that: she was a daughter protecting her father.

He stood on the street, hardly aware of passersby. He wondered if he might be putting himself in danger, barging in and asking questions whose answers were risky. Was he pulling at threads that would unravel stories of fire, thousands of pounds' worth of destruction, deceit, possibly even a death . . . and a fortune made and lost in one night?

What if the Customs men—always a presence on the docks—had seen Crowe visit Prism's office and asked the man about their conversation? Prism would not willingly betray the doctor, but his fear could give him away. At least Crowe had been able to question him. But he told himself that he must be more careful. He must ask questions for a reason that was easy to accept . . . and to believe. And he needed to avoid putting anyone at risk for answering his questions.

As for this fire, what had the River Police done about it? He could not believe that Monk had turned his back on arson, even less on murder. Had something stopped him? Lack of proof? Or was he building a case slowly, not one based on a simple theft or fraud, but murder? And yet, so much time had passed.

Crowe wondered if his questions might in some way endanger Monk's investigation. He did not see how, but even if there was some truth to that, it would not stop him. He had to protect Ellie.

He thought of looking into records of tides, shipments, and fires, rather than asking people. It might
take longer, but if his questions endangered Ellie, or
her family, that might be the better option. The problem
was that he wasn't sure which route to take. Direct
questions could provide the kind of information he
might not be able to find in documents; indirect questions might take him in too many directions, most of
them wrong.

It was easy enough to check the date of the fire that
had destroyed Hollister's warehouse. And he was certain that he'd find the list of goods lost by Silas Dolan.

One trip to the library was all it took. There, he
found old newspapers that gave him all the information
made available to the public. More than the date of the
fire and the amount of damage, Crowe was able to put
together a good estimate of the cost of the goods destroyed, how many fire engines had attended the fire,
and how long it had raged. The stories of individual
courage moved him deeply. Would he have been so
brave? He read about the man who had died, a simple
man, a warehouse worker trapped in the flames. He
had a family, innocents left without the wages that kept
them alive.

The most important fact around this fire was that

someone had died. He had to remind himself to focus on this. If it was arson, it was also murder.

He could have made notes of it all, but his memory was so well trained that he needed neither words nor notes to remind him.

$C$rowe went back to the clinic that afternoon and was surprised by Scuff's wide smile. The young man had not only made a list of medicines and supplies they needed, but he had put them in order of urgency and frequent use. He handed the list to Crowe.

Crowe studied the list, which was depressingly long. It had been a while since they had helped patients who had more than the barest of necessities to spare. Instead of money, they gave food, and even that was often more than they could afford. Many evenings, Crowe had the terrible feeling that he was eating someone else's dinner. One time, when he had accepted a slab of ham from a patient in return for treatment, Scuff had looked at him questioningly.

"If we don't accept their food," Crowe had explained later, "or any gift, for that matter, people will lose their dignity. And if that happens, they might feel as if they could not come to the clinic again. And when they finally do come," he had added, "it could be too late."

Scuff had understood.

Crowe took the list and shook out money from the cash jar, and then he left. This time, he went closer to the shoreline. There were peddlers there who knew far more than they ever said. Crowe knew that they had to be wise and careful to scratch a living in the streets every day, and to sleep in something better than a doorway on a winter night.

He found a news vendor down near the wharf. A barge had just been unloaded and the goods were piled up, waiting on the porters and stevedores to divide it all, then reload everything onto wagons, carts, and some smaller flat barges going up the river to shallower water. He knew that this vendor would sell no newspapers to anyone until the laborers, his primary customers, were through with their work.

"Cup of tea, Spike?" Crowe asked.

The man's face lit up. He knew Crowe's offer was serious, and that the tea would probably have a bun of some sort to go with it. It might even include a place to sit down out of the biting wind off the river, which was damp and edged with ice.

Spike nodded slowly. "You want to know summink?" He stood straighter, as if realizing he was about to do something important.

He was a tall man, wiry, with a shock of red hair shoved off his face, reminding Crowe of one of those scarecrows propped up in fields to warn away the birds. "Of course," Crowe replied.

"And you tell me nothing, right?" The question was sharp, but his eyes were smiling. "You keep a doctor's silence, even when you're not being a doctor. You want it every which way."

"I do," Crowe agreed with a shrug and a smile. "Let's argue about it over tea. Somewhere warm." He turned and led Spike toward a cauldron of hot tea that stood fifty yards away. There was a broken wall another fifty yards beyond that, and shelter behind it. Crowe bought the last three buns as well.

Spike ate one of the fresh buns completely before even speaking to Crowe. "Yeah?" he said, looking carefully at his mug of steaming tea. "What you wanna know?"

"The fire," Crowe replied. "Not quite a year ago. Warehouse on Tooley Street."

Spike's mouth turned down at the corners. "Nasty. Very nasty. Even if it weren't on purpose, bad stuff."

"Is there any good stuff in a fire?" Crowe kept his expression neutral. "Lost a lot of stuff in this one. Fabrics?"

Spike gave him a tired look, as if his patience was being strained to breaking. "Losing your grip, are you? Don't be daft! A few bolts, that's all. Some of 'em scorched a bit around the edges." He shook his head, his eyes steady on Crowe's face. "You're putting me on, Doc. What is it really? Is it about Maddock?"

Crowe had to look as if he understood. Maddock? For a moment he could not place the name, but there was an ugly thought taking shape in his mind, a dark shape heavy with fear. Maddock was the name he had read in the newspaper, the night watchman who had burned to death in the fire. Crowe nodded, tightening his lips, trying not to show too much emotion.

He must have failed because Spike said, "Yeah, poor sod, that Maddock." His voice was bitter. "You wanna see his bones?" Spike said bitterly. "They burned them. What does it matter to you that he's dead?"

It was what Crowe had feared, at the back of his mind. The dreadful shape he refused to look at. And was that what Ellie feared? That her father was somehow responsible for Maddock's death? Of course, she would not tell Crowe of her fears. She probably would not even allow herself to acknowledge them. What could she do, other than accept the price—that she was being married off to this brute in order to keep Silas and Paul Dolan quiet? Did she even know if it was true? Had Hollister admitted his role in this arson to her, telling her what she must do to save his life? If he were convicted of arson, and a man had burned to death in that fire, they would hang him.

Even after all this time, could it be the reason Monk had not acted yet? It was a capital crime, so it would take intensive, and possibly lengthy, investigating. William Monk would never let such an important possibility as death by arson slide by. Whoever was found guilty would face the gallows. If Monk got it wrong and hanged an innocent man, it would be impossible to undo. The man would be dead, and the Lords Justices would be loath to admit their error. Very loath indeed.

Crowe believed he knew Ellie. At least, there was a side of her that he felt he knew. That was her ability to face pain and endure it without complaint. He had watched her do so, despite her fear and suffering. He saw how determined she was that if she cried, she would do so when she thought no one was watching.

As before, he longed to comfort her now, even share the weight of her pain, but it would break a barrier that had to exist between them. He was her doctor; she was his patient. It was possible that, to her, he could never be more than that.

How could he help her? How could he be sure that seeking the truth might not make matters worse? He could do nothing without discovering all the information that was available regarding the fire. He had so much yet to learn. Perhaps most importantly, he needed to uncover who had set it. Was it someone who would profit from it? Or perhaps someone paid to do the job, an expert. Arson was a skill, an art. Who else knew the truth about it? What was their interest, and their price for silence?

The place to start was finding out who had taken the bales of wool, silk, and those valuable furs out of the warehouse before the fire was set. Who received the insurance money? Joe had told him that it would be Hollister and Dolan, each man taking his share.

There were other questions rolling through Crowe's mind, questions that might be harder to answer. How carefully had the insurance company investigated the fire? And if they didn't do a thorough investigation, was someone in that insurance company part of the plot? And if so, what was their share?

One more question rushed into his head: Did the insurance adjuster have ties to Hollister or to Dolan? Powerful men often relied on those of lower status to do their dirty work.

Of course, there was one other very important question that he needed to explore. What could he learn about Maddock, the man who died?

No matter how excellent his memory, Crowe knew that he must make a list of all these questions, and then tick them off when he found the answers. He would make a plan, although it might be altered with every new fact learned.

Whatever he did, and whatever he learned, he knew it was a nightmare that must be faced. But he was determined to understand why someone as gentle as Ellie would agree to marry a bully like Paul Dolan. Everything he was being told brought him closer to his suspicions. It was not to please her father, but to protect him. If she knew about the black shadow of guilt hanging over him, or even suspected it, that could be explanation enough.

But where was the justice in that? A young woman forced into a loveless marriage.

Injustice was like an acid burning into him. Maddock had been killed. Silas Dolan and his son had grown rich. So had Albert Hollister. But perhaps Hollister's enhanced wealth came with the constant fear that the Dolans could expose him anytime they chose. Could they? But then, by exposing him, were they not also exposing themselves? Or was it only the fear of that possibility that gripped Hollister by the throat and choked the courage out of him?

Crowe knew he was getting closer to the truth, but what would he do when he found it? Not just the Dolans, but also Hollister could end up in prison! Was it possible for Silas Dolan to prove Hollister's part in the insurance fraud without implicating himself or his son? If that was so, and if Dolan was that clever, then it must follow that even if Hollister was found guilty, he could not take Dolan down with him.

Crowe ran these thoughts through his mind. One man blackmailing a second man to be his partner in crime? What if Silas Dolan was not guilty, but he knew that Hollister was? No, it was more likely that he had covered his tracks so carefully that even if Hollister knew the truth and was willing to implicate Dolan, he could not prove it. Was it even believable that Dolan could be a blackmailer, but not a thief or an arsonist?

Finding the truth was vital, but he had to proceed with caution. If he made a mistake and blamed Hollister alone, then Ellie would be disgraced, left high and dry. She would live with shame and guilt, and no home. Even worse, she would watch her father tried before a jury and, in all probability, hanged. Crowe wondered if he would rather Dolan got away with these crimes than have that happen to Ellie's father.

Of course, there was the possibility that Hollister was not guilty of anything. The whole plot could have been devised by Silas Dolan. That might be so, but Hollister certainly must have played some part in the plan. Why else allow Ellie to marry Paul Dolan? Even more, force her into it?

Crowe had to ask himself if he carried another fear, even darker and more chilling, in the back of his mind. Could Ellie have been party to this sinister plot? Not that she was there when the crime was committed, but had known what had transpired and had kept silent, out of fear for her father's reputation, or perhaps even his safety. Could Crowe honestly expect her to be entirely innocent? What would the Dolans or her father do to her if she fought against them, even threatened to tell? And tell who? The police? Why would they believe her? Who would protect her from the Dolans, or even her father, if these men decided to silence her before she spoke up?

Crowe could not deny that even the people we love

most possess human frailties. They're all vulnerable, and they have weaknesses to overcome. Isn't that what life is for? Not to conquer others, but to conquer those flaws in ourselves?

He bought Spike another cup of tea, sat with him, and watched as he ate the third bun. He reached into his pocket for a piece of paper and pulled out Scuff's list of supplies the clinic needed. He would buy all of them before heading back.

Crowe now understood that it would require all his attention to deal with Hollister and the Dolans, and his time was limited. Once Ellie was married to Paul Dolan, the problem would become unsolvable. And with Christmas less than a week away, it might be more difficult to find the people who held the answers.

$\mathcal{S}$cuff understood the compulsion that drove Crowe to learn more about Ellie's family, and the urgency of knowing the facts before it was too late. Crowe had shared some of what he knew about the fire, and Scuff knew that his mentor would not give up seeking the truth, especially where Ellie Hollister's safety was involved. Her safety . . . and her happiness.

Scuff continued organizing the treatment room, making certain that they had what was needed. He had been living and working in the clinic for over two years now and he knew the daily routines. He also appreciated that Crowe had taught him every possible skill he could, first by having him watch, and then by copying as Crowe critiqued him. And then, lastly, by doing it himself. This last step—learning from hands-on experience—was beginning earlier than either of them had expected, but it was because Crowe's need to help Ellie did not wait upon anyone else's timing.

Having this responsibility left Scuff racked with nerves. At the same time, he would have been disappointed had Crowe not asked him to help. Now, with so much responsibility, he had to think hard and ask himself complicated questions, in order to understand certain medical techniques used by Crowe. When it came to moral decisions, however, Scuff was never confused. Crowe had taught him well.

He thought of those times when he had sat up with Ellie when she was in pain, and Crowe was so exhausted that he had no choice but to sleep. Scuff had watched him change her bandages, and had then done it himself. There were times when Scuff slept in the afternoon, and then sat through the long night with her.

Crowe had never spoken about his feelings for her,

but Scuff understood them, and understood hers also. Could they ever share more than a mutual trust, along with their efforts required for her healing? For Crowe's sake, he hoped they could.

So, it was no surprise when Crowe had awakened him earlier that morning to say that he was leaving to learn all he could about Hollister and Dolan. He gave Scuff the list of duties that should be handled in his absence. There was no way to foresee which patients might come, but Crowe trusted Scuff to do whatever must be done. He knew that Scuff had the skills. All he needed was the confidence . . . and the courage. Along with the list, Crowe gave him a quick pat on the shoulder, then he left, going out into the brisk December wind off the river, and the sunlight on the wet roads.

As much as he had wanted to, Scuff was not able to go back to sleep. Once he'd had a quick breakfast, including three cups of tea, he focused on the small jobs to do, things that were often put off because patients arrived and were in need of attention. Sometimes, there were so many in need that he felt a bit overwhelmed.

Now, however, he wished for patients. Nothing serious, perhaps a cut to stitch, or a deep splinter to remove, something to bandage and strap up. Perhaps someone with dust in the eye that needed to be washed out. Or someone to comfort, reassure. In fact, he would like to have had anyone call by, simply to talk to. He was so used to being rushed that he felt quite useless when doing things that did not really need to be done with any urgency.

On the other hand, there was no pleasure in seeing pain, even if he was able to ease it.

A dock laborer came in with a deep cut in his arm. Scuff was able to clean it thoroughly, and then stitch it up and reassure the man that he would soon heal. Scuff was grateful that it was the kind of injury he'd seen before, and not something that he felt was beyond his expertise.

When he was finished treating the wound, the man was relieved, all anxiety gone, and with only residual pain remaining. He promised to come back with money for the clinic.

Scuff acknowledged his offer. Probably, he would fulfill his promise. It was Scuff's experience that very few people failed to contribute what they were able to.

He cleared up the instruments, placed all the bandages in the cupboard, then scrubbed the floor and put the bucket and scrubbing brush away. With no patients in the clinic, silence returned.

Scuff was aware of feeling lonely.

He had lunch early, not because he was hungry so much as he was bored.

He decided to study, and had just pulled out one of the more serious medical books when there was a peremptory knock on the door and two policemen came in. In fact, they pushed the door open before Scuff could answer them.

The larger of the two had the dark shadow of a beard, even so early in the afternoon. When he introduced himself and his junior companion, his voice was quiet, unusually soft for a man of his size. He looked Scuff up and down, noting his casual attire, including trousers worn at the knees and held up by a leather belt because they were two sizes too large, and his lopsided shirt collar poking above the heavy sweater he wore for warmth. And, of course, his well-darned socks.

"Do you work here?" the sergeant asked, still scanning him.

Scuff resented the attitude. He realized that his clothing made him look far from impressive, but he was tall and stood very straight. He was nearly the same height as the sergeant, and taller than the constable standing beside him. "Yes," Scuff answered simply.

He was not afraid of the police. William Monk, his adoptive father, his closest friend, except perhaps for his adoptive mother, was not only a policeman but head of the Thames River Police, and a man known throughout London . . . and sometimes feared, with reason.

Scuff looked the sergeant straight in the eye. Not with insolence, but not with fear either—at least he hoped not. He had done nothing wrong. As an apprentice, he was allowed to perform simple tasks, but he knew that there were also limitations. He never asked for information as to how an injury had occurred, except what was necessary to treat it, and he guarded what he was told as a confidence. A doctor could work no other way.

"Doing what?" the sergeant asked, one eyebrow raised slightly. It gave his face a skeptical look.

"Helping Dr. Crowe," Scuff answered.

A look of impatience crossed the sergeant's face. "With? Sweeping floors, washing dishes, rolling bandages, carrying out the rubbish, shopping for . . . whatever? Bandages, medicines . . ."

Scuff was stung. Was the man being deliberately insulting? Crowe had warned him not to lose his temper. It was the old police trick, leading someone into striking the first blow. When you lost your temper, however provoked, you lost control. "If necessary, yes," he said. He must be careful. He was not yet qualified. "But anyone can do that. I also perform minor operations, stitch up wounds, give medicines. And if we have a serious operation to perform, I assist him with that. Pass him things, instruments, thread needles." He kept his voice level. "I learn a lot from him."

"So, you're a doctor, then? A real one? Or just the best you can do around here?" It was the younger man who spoke, the constable. He had a soft face, but not gentle, just hinting at loose jowls when he got older, and when he put on a little weight.

Scuff kept his temper with difficulty. "I'm taking courses in medicine, and I'm also learning a lot from Dr. Crowe." He took a breath. "He does the skilled stuff, of course. I watch and learn."

The sergeant looked around the room. "And where is he, then, this real doctor?"

Scuff's mind raced as to what he should say. Why had they come anyway? What would send them away satisfied? And what could he say that might only earn more trouble? What might prove to be untrue, as they looked into it later? Truth was the safest, always. "I don't know, sir. Dr. Crowe was going to look into the progress of a patient he attended some while ago. I don't know where he was intending to go after that. He should be back later, if you care to wait."

"So, you refuse to say?" the constable said sharply.

Scuff swallowed hard. They were trying to provoke him. "I don't expect him to account to me where he goes. A patient's home address, or what the trouble is, is not my business. I'm sure if he attended you, or your wife, for something private, you would not wish him to discuss it with the neighbors. Or even with me. Whatever the situation, it would grow in the telling."

The constable raised his eyebrows cynically. "And you don't discuss it at all? Curious. Then how do you learn? Isn't that what you say you are here for?"

"Yes, sir. I'll learn the rules as well as the treatment. That's what I'm trying to tell you." He saw the anger on the sergeant's face.

The constable snapped. "As police, we have the right to ask questions. And it's your duty to answer them! Now . . . where is Crowe?"

Scuff took a deep breath and let it out slowly. "I've told you, sir, I don't know. He started out to make inquiries about a patient from a while ago, a lady."

"And what was a lady doing coming to a place like this, eh? Wouldn't she have her own doctor? Is something going on 'ere that a real doctor wouldn't do?"

Scuff knew what he meant. Rage welled up inside him. And at the same time, a growing fear all but suffocated him. Who had sent this man? What was he really after? Punishing Crowe for some imaginary offense, perhaps related to his inquiries into the arson in the warehouse? Or the death of the night watchman? He felt the chill deep inside himself.

"No, it was a street accident, and not far from here," he answered, watching the man's face. "She was bleeding very badly from a leg wound." He took a deep breath and nearly choked. "The wound needed immediate attention. I can say nothing more. I've taken an oath."

He should not have mentioned this, he knew, but the accusation that Crowe was doing illegal things, such as helping women terminate pregnancies, made him sick. "She was a lady," he went on. "And I can only imagine what her father would say if he knew what you're suggesting. He would have his servants thrash you till you needed a pretty good surgeon to put you back together again. That is, if they could find all the pieces."

The sergeant looked startled, while his young constable reached out as if to grab Scuff by the shoulders. "I'll have you for that," the older man said between his teeth.

At that moment, a voice called out from the room behind them. "Help! Is someone there? He's bad! Can't . . . I can't get it out!"

Scuff pushed the sergeant out of the way and rushed to the old man and the boy now standing in the doorway. The boy was white-faced and holding up his wrist, which was bleeding freely, scarlet running down his hand and dripping onto the floor. Scuff could see torn flesh and the shaft of a large fishhook buried deep in the tissue.

"Yes, I'm here," Scuff said firmly. "We'll get that out and stop the bleeding. Don't worry." He wasn't sure he could do this, but he meant to try. "Hold it up," he told the boy, indicating how he should raise his arm. "It'll help slow the bleeding."

He pushed past the police and led the boy to the chair in the main room used for patients. He looked at the old man. "Hang on to him. Don't want him to faint and fall." He turned to the sergeant. "You can help while you are here. See there, the basin. Put hot water in it and hold it still, then take these scissors and cut his sleeve away so I can get to the hook." When the sergeant didn't move, he said, "Don't stand there, man! I've got to get a needle and thread, and a knife to cut the hook free."

The sergeant remained frozen.

Scuff swung toward the constable. "Are you any use, then?"

"I'll do it!" the sergeant said, his voice hoarse. He went to where Scuff was pointing to fetch the basin, and then to the stove, which was always burning, where he pushed the pot of water onto the hottest part.

Scuff knew exactly where all his instruments were: the sterilized and sharpest scalpel, the needle already threaded through the eye with the finest gut, almost as fine as a hair, and plenty of bandages.

"Give me that bottle," he ordered the constable, pointing at the medical spirits above the stove.

He smiled at the old man. "Hold on to him. You won't pass out, will you?"

The old man swallowed hard. "No, sir, I— No, I won't."

Scuff gave him a quick smile. "Good." He did not even glance at either of the policemen. Instead, he concentrated on the fishhook, and the flesh it was embedded in.

The boy was not watching. Clearly, he did not wish to see, and Scuff could not blame him for that. The wound was a mess, and still bleeding, but more slowly now.

He needed a little help. He looked at the constable. "Will you please give me a hand? Fetch me the things I ask for."

The constable froze. "I dunno, I—"

Scuff forced himself to smile more directly. "You're not refusing, are you?"

"No!" Reluctantly, he shook his head, so small a gesture as to be barely visible.

"Thank you." Scuff held out a dry cloth. "Soak this in the hot water," he said, pointing to the bowl of hot water now at his elbow. "And then pass it to me when I say."

"Right!"

Scuff took another slow breath. He had two choices: he could try to work slowly, tearing as little flesh as possible, which might be easier for him, but would hurt the boy appallingly, or he could cut the flesh open quickly and remove the hook, and then sew the gap as soon as possible. Above all, he needed to hold the scalpel steadily, and not let the boy cringe so violently that a vein could be severed. "Hold tight," he said to the boy. Then he glanced at the old man, and nodded.

Scuff deliberately tightened his grip on the blade, then eased it a little as he cut the flesh to get the hook out. As soon as it was free, he moved quickly to stop the bleeding, watching closely so he could stanch the flow and keep the area around the wound clean. He let it bleed a little more, to be sure there were no pieces of metal or dirt or anything else in the wound, then he took the bottle of spirits and poured a bit over the wound. Confident that it was clean, he gestured to the policeman, took the soaked cloth, and then swabbed the area again.

He bent over the wound as he stitched it up, concentrating intensely. He wondered if he was putting in more stitches than were needed. Crowe would have done it better, more neatly. He must be careful not to make the sutures too tight. That would make it hurt even more. "Another swab," he said to the constable.

The constable hesitated, then obeyed.

Scuff could see that this was not unwillingness, but the beginning of appreciation for what they were doing.

Scuff took the swab. "Thank you. Nearly finished," he said to the boy. "Can you keep it still just a little longer?"

The boy nodded, his lips pursed tightly, tears filling his eyes.

"It'll hurt," Scuff warned. "You might have a scar there. Would you mind that? Having a battle scar?"

"Will I? You reckon?" There was a hint of hope in the boy's voice. What little boy didn't want a battle scar!

"Yes," Scuff said with certainty, although he had no idea. "Hold still, last thing and we're done." He actually had quite a lot more to do, but the boy was looking at him, not at the wound, which had almost stopped bleeding.

The constable was watching just as closely. He picked the right moment to hand over another clean swab.

The old man still held on to the boy. Scuff could see that he was less tense, his hand resting gently on the boy's shoulder.

Scuff continued to work as quickly as he could, but carefully.

There was silence in the room. The sergeant was still standing in exactly the same place, watching. What was he going to do when Scuff was finished? Ask more about Crowe? Scuff realized that he had an idea why these men were here. It was to do with Ellie, and with Silas Dolan. What did they want from Crowe? Just to warn him? How did they know Crowe was asking questions? And how could Scuff protect him? He thought about the warehouse fire, and the death of a man, and he knew that those events were the reason why Crowe kept rushing off. He hoped these policemen wouldn't ask him again to explain Crowe's absence. Or was the officer going to ask about the fire, or the goods that had been burned? Or not! Or about someone Crowe had treated. Scuff would not answer, even if he knew.

The sergeant was moving from foot to foot, his impatience growing.

Scuff tied off the last of the sutures and then cut the remaining thread. Finally, he wrapped a bandage around it. "You come back tomorrow, just to be sure," he told the boy. "And don't get it wet. Keep it as clean as you can."

"Thank you," the boy said carefully, pronouncing the words as if he were unused to the weight of them.

"You're welcome," Scuff replied, releasing the boy's arm and sitting back in his chair. His shoulders were tight from the tension of heavy concentration. And the presence of these policemen was adding to it.

The old man regarded Scuff carefully, then pulled a package out of his pocket. It was wrapped in old newspaper, and pretty wet. "We caught this earlier," he said. He placed it on the bench. It was not necessary to explain that it was a fish. "You know how to cook it?" He looked at Scuff skeptically.

"I do, yes, thank you," Scuff replied. "I like fish. That'll pay nicely for this treatment. And for coming back tomorrow, too, so be sure you do!"

"You always need to do your work twice?" the old man asked.

"As many times as necessary to make sure everything is healing." Scuff realized that his hands were clenched because, without Crowe's presence, he was still unsure of himself. With his presence, Scuff wouldn't have given it a second thought.

The old man grunted, then took the boy very gently by the shoulder and turned him round to face the door.

"You sure that's going to get better?" the sergeant asked dubiously, as soon as the old man and the child were out of the door. "That how you eat? You get stuff from people like that?"

"Sometimes." Scuff looked at the constable. "Thank you for your help."

The constable was smiling. Perhaps he did not mean to, but it was clear he could not remove that expression from his face. "How did you learn to do that?" he asked.

Scuff smiled back. "Most of it from Dr. Crowe, but also from my adoptive mother." He did not know why he added that. Probably it was so they wouldn't think Hester was the sort of woman whose child was a mudlark, left to fend for himself along the riverbank. "She was a nurse in the Crimea and often did the duties of a doctor when there was not one there."

The sergeant looked at him with some disbelief. He could see that Scuff was clever. And his hands were carefully scrubbed. "So, you came to work for Crowe?"

He gestured as if dismissing the idea. "Does this mother of yours approve of that?"

The contempt Scuff heard in his voice was ugly. In fact, it scalded like a burn on tender flesh. He knew he was vulnerable, and how every callous or degrading word caught him. "I wouldn't do it if she didn't!" he snapped. "And, in case you didn't realize it, many doctors don't ask who you are or whether you can pay. They ask what you need, where it hurts, and how it happened."

The sergeant scowled. "Your mother isn't a doctor, boy. Women don't do that. They ain't got the—" He thought again before he chose the word. "They ain't suited to it."

"Even to save the life of a soldier?" Scuff asked, knowing he should back out of this before it got any worse. "Have you seen the sort of wounds they get in the army?"

"What's that got to do with anything?" The sergeant seemed to feel on safer ground again. It was in his face, and the angle of his shoulders.

"Because if you had," Scuff glared at him, "you'd have heard of Florence Nightingale, and you would show your respect for the women who left the comfort of their homes and went out to the Crimea and nursed on the battlefield, not just in the hospitals. They dealt with fevers and men dying every day. Limbs blown off and limbs amputated. They had more courage than most doctors who sleep in their beds all night."

"That's why you want to be a doctor?" the sergeant asked. "Because of her?"

"Yes." Scuff didn't know if it was or not, but probably it was. When he was younger, on the riverbank, where he had first met Monk, he wanted to be like Monk. A policeman! Someone who was strong, who never backed down from anyone or anything. Who was never afraid, at least not so you'd know it. Then Monk had taken him to his home, and let him stay there. That was where Scuff had met Hester. He wasn't used to women, and he was not at all sure that he liked her. He knew that she would want to make him clean up, wash his hair. She would expect him to learn how to speak properly, and how to sit at a table and use a knife and fork. She might treat him like he couldn't look after himself! Tell him what to do, when to go to bed, when to get up . . . and make him wash!

Except that Hester Monk wasn't like that. And she never tried to hug him! Actually, it was he who had first hugged her. And that was when he had been horribly frightened—it was an experience he did not want to think of even now—and he was already six feet tall and perfectly able to defend himself. He remembered how Hester had treated him quite casually, not like a child, but more like a friend.

She would expect him to treat these policemen civilly, using his intelligence and self-control, and not his temper. Not that Hester never lost her self-control! He had seen her angry—furious, in fact—and he had seen her weep. But never while someone needed treatment, help, skill. Only her family—and that was William Monk and Scuff—knew how deep her pain went.

Nothing he could think of would hurt her more than for him to revert to the riverbank urchin he once had been, instead of the man she had taught him to become.

He looked at the sergeant. "Why do you ask why I wanted to become a doctor, Sergeant?"

"It matters not why! You will answer my questions," the sergeant snapped. "Or I'll close this place down! Do you hear me?"

Scuff stood very straight, his mind racing. He had thought the sergeant was coming round, but here he was, biting, bullying. Perhaps he wasn't interested in Scuff's career decisions, but was reacting to the pressure put on him to get his hands on Crowe.

Crowe had left Scuff in charge, but what would he do

when faced with this? Not provoke a fight, that was for certain. But not give in either.

"What are your questions?" Scuff said as civilly as he could, but he heard the edge in his voice, the challenge. "You saw what I did for that boy, and you know as much about him as I do. You know exactly what he paid me. We get lots of people like that." Was he avoiding the question? He wasn't sure.

"Women come in, too?" the sergeant asked, suspicion in his voice.

"Whoever comes gets treated," Scuff said. "But if it's to do with birthing and such, we have midwives who do that. They're used to it, and the women are more comfortable having other women taking care of them."

"Always?" the sergeant pressed. "Midwives always do this?"

"As far as I know. Why? Are you're asking about someone special?"

"Checking a few stories I've heard," the sergeant said, looking him straight in the eye.

Scuff looked straight back, far more boldly than he felt. "Well, I'm not telling you any more details of our patients' illnesses," he answered. "You want to know about women and their ailments, then ask them. I wouldn't tell you, even if I knew."

The sergeant flushed, as if this upstart Scuff had accused him of something dirty. "You better watch yourself, young man. I can close you down, and don't you forget that!"

It was a very real threat. Scuff felt a chill inside him, just thinking of the number of people he would be letting down if this happened. People needed this clinic to help them when they were ill or injured. They depended on Crowe's advice, and trusted that he knew what he was doing. Which was to take away the pain and the fear, if it was humanly possible. Crowe, who always had patience for them, who never panicked, however bad it looked. And who believed fervently that it was wrong to betray a confidence.

And there was another element to this: Crowe trusted Scuff. And for Scuff, this was a lot to live up to. Was he doing that? Or was he buckling under the pressure? And a slight pressure at that, which was caused by the offensiveness of a man who was also insulting him. He knew that Crowe would have dealt with it better. He was certain it was Crowe they were after, but why? Because he was looking into the warehouse fire, and that upset Dolan, and perhaps Ellie's father?

He drew in a deep breath. "People trust us not to talk about them or their private affairs, their illnesses. They come here, knowing we will do anything we can to help." He had already argued this point, but the sergeant wouldn't let it go. "I wouldn't talk about you to others," said Scuff. "And that includes if you had an accident near here, and I was the doctor to help you."

The constable was staring at him, as if Scuff were the only person in the room. And it was a look of respect, Scuff was quite certain of that. This strengthened his resolve. He was not going to let himself be provoked into being less than who he was taught to be, and all because this bully of a sergeant did not feel the same. It was Scuff's choice to determine how he behaved; he refused to give any power to the sergeant. "Dr. Crowe isn't here right now, and I don't know where he is or when he'll be back. Now, if you'll excuse me, I've got to clean up and be ready in case someone else needs help."

"And if they don't?" the sergeant asked. "You going to stand here waiting?"

"No, I'm going to get my books out and study."

"What did you say your name was, again?" the sergeant asked.

Scuff stood very straight. He had never had a real name until Monk and Hester had adopted him. At first, he had not wanted to be adopted. It felt like he was giving up his right to choose for himself, even giving up his identity. Then he had been kidnapped, and rescued. Perhaps Monk would have rescued all the boys, because that sort of thing was his job, but he also knew, for the first time deep into his bones, that to Monk and Hester he was special. The people on the riverbank called him Scuff. Living there, he had been totally free and did not belong to anybody! But then, nobody had ever come looking for him, even at the risk of their own lives. People might know where he was, but that was not at all the same thing as being sought and then found. And Monk and Hester had, indeed, found him. After that, the idea of being adopted felt right. The Monks always cared where he was, and treated him so that he never felt as if he were giving away a part of himself. And that was good. In fact, it was very good!

Of course, there was a price, which was mostly obedience. The caring bit, the minding what they thought of him, came whether he wanted it or not. Slowly, he had felt part of this new family.

Then, one day, he had been to church with Hester. Church was frankly a bit of a bore, and kind of ridiculous. And he had to dress up for it. No one minded that he had been poor, lots of the people were, but they minded if he didn't have a proper haircut, and clean dark clothes, and shoes! It didn't matter if his clothing was a little too big or too small, and nobody noticed patches or a hole here and there. Even his trousers, a bit short in the leg, went unnoticed. But heaven help him if he didn't have a clean handkerchief!

So, he went with Hester, and it felt nice. She always had something interesting to say about the people around them, though he wasn't allowed to repeat it. She could see right through people, just as he could, but in a different way. Especially self-important people. But then, she was a nurse. She knew people were all made the same way, underneath the black jackets with fur collars, and the black bombazine dresses. Good word that: bombazine! Stiff, black, self-important. People were fragile all in their own ways.

He had been introduced to the minister, who was wearing what Scuff first thought was a long black dress, except that it wasn't a dress, it was a cassock! When the minister asked Scuff his name, Scuff couldn't say . . . because he didn't know. He didn't have a proper name!

It was Hester who answered. "This is Will Monk," she said. But then, if she were his mother, and his father was head of the Thames River Police, it was his name by right, not like he had borrowed it.

He still thought of himself as Scuff, but that was just a name to call him by, for anyone who knew him well. To others, he was Will Monk, and one day he would be Dr. Monk. Hester would really be proud of him then! Even Monk himself would like that.

He answered the sergeant. "I'm Will Monk."

The sergeant thought about that for a moment or two, and then wrote something in his notebook. After telling the constable to pay attention, they both left the clinic. But just before the constable walked onto the street, he turned round and gave Scuff a smile. A real one. Not just to put on the show.

It was then that Scuff realized that the man had linked him to William Monk, his father, the head of Thames River Police.

Scuff smiled back at him.

*S*cuff was putting away newly washed pots and pans when he heard a noise. He turned to see who was there. Crowe had told him of Mattie, the little girl from a few days ago. This must be her. And this time she was not alone. She held in her arms, rather too tightly, a calico and white cat, very small. A kitten, in fact.

"I brung you a present," she said, looking up at Scuff.

She unfastened the kitten's claws from her sleeve and held it out.

For a moment, Scuff froze. "It's very little," he stated.

"She'll grow," Mattie replied. "Her name is Rosie. She'll catch mices for you, and rats."

What on earth could he say? The little creature, barely weeks old, was wriggling and likely to fall. He took it from her and held it in his arms. It fastened its needle-like claws into his woolen sweater. When he put his hand around the kitten to make sure he had hold of her, she started to purr. Her whole body was vibrating, and her blue eyes were closed in pleasure.

"Rosie," he repeated. He didn't want a cat. He had no time to look after a baby animal.

"She likes you," Mattie said with a shy smile.

"Are you sure it's a she?" he asked. Not that it mattered, but it was something to say while he thought about the best way to handle this.

"Always are, when they're this color," said Mattie. "She'll grow up to be a good mouser!"

He had no idea if that was true, but it sounded reasonable. He swallowed hard. Here was this child, with no apparent family, giving him probably the most precious thing she had—her friend, a tiny cat who was as alone and as dependent as she was. Without thinking, he stroked the soft little head. It would need milk every day! And what else? Meat? It was far too small to catch any mouse at all, let alone one that was big enough to feed it.

Mattie watched him, her eyes full of trust, but slowly her expression changed. Scuff was certain she was realizing that perhaps he didn't see the kitten as the same precious thing that she did.

"You have to come here and feed her for me." Scuff heard his own voice and could barely believe it. What was he doing?

"I can do that!" she said, her face shining with hope again. "I'll look after her all the time."

He felt the heat rising up his face. "We'll find a place for her to sleep. Are you sure she won't run away?"

"No, she won't," Mattie said with certainty. "Not if you feed her." She looked at him curiously. She was a child of the streets, he could see it in her eyes, hear it in her voice. He should recognize it! He had been about her age when he first spent a night on the riverbank, cold, hungry, and alone.

"If I get some milk now, will you feed her for me?" he asked.

Mattie nodded vigorously. She clearly wanted to say something more, but it seemed as if she dared not.

Scuff knew that there would never be any way he could go back on this now. Crowe would be furious. And yet, while he thought this, he could quite clearly hear himself say, "Mattie, you'll have to stay here, or at least come very often. Would your mother allow you to do that?"

Mattie gave a tiny shrug. "She won't know. She's gone."

"Where are you staying?" he asked, then immediately wondered if this was a mistake. He plunged on, looking at her as her eyes brimmed with tears. She had offered him her companion, this kitten, another hungry and lonely child! "Then do you think you could stay here? If I found a place for you near the stove, and a blanket? Then Rosie could sleep there, too?" He waited, as if it were really a question that she alone could answer. He wanted to kick himself for not having offered this sooner. Another lesson learned about making decisions.

Her eyes widened. "I think I could do that. It will be good . . . for Rosie."

"Yes, it would," he answered. "And then I wouldn't worry about her. If you really mean that she's mine. You could help me for a little while anyway, if you don't mind."

"I don't mind." she said solemnly, then gave him a sweet smile. She put up her arms to take the kitten from him. "Have you got any milk?" she asked.

While he fetched milk and a little dish, he put to the back of his mind every possible explanation he could make to Crowe as to why there was no milk left, and possibly only one egg. And why there was a very small girl, still with her own milk teeth, asleep on the floor beside the kitchen stove, and a very small cat, also with milk teeth that were sharp like a row of pins.

"Once she's fed, we'll change those bandages of yours," Scuff told the girl. She nodded in agreement without looking away from the small creature.

*I*t was late afternoon and Crowe had learned all he could about Hollister, and the fire that had changed his fortunes and those of Silas Dolan, as well as having taken the life of Maddock, the night watchman. He knew he could no longer avoid learning the truth as to why there had been no prosecution. The insurance company had apparently paid out in full, and both Hollister and Dolan were better off than they had been before.

Again, he wondered if the Thames River Police—and more specifically, William Monk—had given up on the case. Perhaps Monk and his team were biding their time, and working at it from some other angle. But it had gone on so long.

Crowe did not want to inquire further with those people he knew. He had already been given a good picture of the blaze itself from a fireman whose family he had once helped.

"No suspicions?" he had asked the man.

The fireman had given him a wide-eyed stare.

"Because I have some," Crowe said.

"Warehouses don't set ablaze all by themselves," said the man. "At least, not often. But it can happen. You take flour, what you make bread with, and it can go off like a bomb; burn down half the street, did you know that?"

"But they weren't storing flour, were they?" Crowe pressed.

"No, there was silks, wool, and furs."

"And did *they* go off like bombs?" Crowe tried to keep the sarcasm out of his voice.

"I ain't saying it was arson," the man replied. "Saying that could get me into real trouble." He leaned closer to Crowe. "But I won't say as it wasn't."

"And if I could read your thoughts?"

The fireman grinned broadly. "You'd say a fine mess, and that they got away clean. But you can't read my thoughts, now, can you!"

"And the night watchman?" Crowe asked bitterly. "What about poor Maddock?"

"Quick death, likely."

"Burning?" Crowe said incredulously. "That's hardly quick."

"Reckon he were probably dead before it started. Professional job, maybe? No matter, I hope he were dead before the fire started. Terrible way to die," he added.

Crowe knew that, as a fireman, he had seen his share of deaths by burning.

"Terrible," the man repeated. "But in these parts, best keep yer mouth shut and stay outa trouble."

"What about the River Police?" Crowe asked. "They'd not have been so easy to fool."

"Don't know. But again, Doc, I can't take ideas to the police if I got no proof. And if I can't prove it, I best not say it. Big man, your Mr. Silas Dolan. Got a lot of people working for 'im."

"But the River Police thought it might be arson?" Crowe asked.

"Who knows what they thought?" The fireman shrugged. "They got different fish to fry. And they got to watch their step, as there's people who got friends in the right places. And Silas Dolan's got some nasty friends. Sometimes a clever man might use one of them friends to catch another, if you see what I mean. But it could take time."

Crowe had seen what he meant, possibly very clearly. Not all police were like Monk, who was not only head of the Thames River Police, but Scuff's adoptive father and friend. He was a clever man, one not to cross, but he was also a man of convictions, not a political climber, and never someone who could be bought with money, or frightened with threats.

Crowe had been putting off the thought of going to Monk, but perhaps now was the time to concede. This time of evening, Monk might still be in his office at Wapping, in the old docks area. Perhaps Crowe stood the best chance of catching him now. Or Monk could have left and would be halfway home. He lived on the south bank, up the hill from the Greenwich ferry. It was not the time of year when anyone spent longer away from home than they had to, especially with Christmas only days away.

Crowe started walking, the resolution forming in his

mind. He was near enough, half a mile, so he headed for the police station. What he didn't want was to make the situation for Ellie even worse. One error, one piece of information that would open the arson case again, and Monk would be compelled to follow it up. As far as Crowe knew, Monk always followed the law, however it affected people. He was not a man to turn a blind eye to anything, except temporarily, and for a reason.

When Crowe found himself standing on the wharf steps leading up to the police station, he could wait no longer. He knew the station would be open all night.

The waterside streets were cold enough up the river, but that was far short of the penetrating chill on the open water. Oilskins were appropriate. He pulled his coat around him, came to the top of the steps, turned the handle, and went in. The warmth of the air wrapped around him like a blanket: soft, almost suffocating.

"Yes, sir?" a constable asked him. The man was not in uniform, and yet his air of confidence said that he belonged here.

Crowe smiled. "My name is Crowe," he began.

"I know who you are, sir. Nothing wrong with Scuff, I hope?" Now there was anxiety in the man's voice, in his eyes.

A CHRISTMAS DELIVERANCE

"He's fine. In fact, he's managing the clinic while I come here. I need Mr. Monk's help."

"Yes, sir. As luck has it, you're catching him before he goes home." He turned and walked quickly to one of the doors leading off the main room. He disappeared, then after a matter of seconds, came back. "This way, sir." He showed Crowe to the office, and left discreetly, closing the door behind him.

Monk was sitting behind his desk. He rose to his feet. He did not ask how Scuff was, but the inquiry was in his keen face. He was a dark, lean man with strong facial bones and steady gray eyes. The touches of white at his temples suited him.

"Scuff is fine," Crowe said, having no time for word games, even for the sake of good manners. Medicine required courtesy, but also speed. "He learns well. I've come about something else, another patient. I think she's in trouble now."

Monk looked surprised, but he pointed to the chair for Crowe to sit down.

"I don't know what you can tell me." Crowe was forestalling the expected refusal on the grounds that Monk could not discuss cases with civilians. Crowe understood that. He had his own laws of confidence. "Some things are public knowledge. That fire just under a year

117

ago, when Albert Hollister's warehouse was burned to the ground. Fortune in wool, silk, and furs destroyed."

"We looked into the insurance claims," Monk said. "And yes, before you ask, they were paid. But how does that concern any patient of yours now?"

"It doesn't," Crowe agreed. It was comfortable and warm in here, but he could not allow himself to relax. "But the watchman was burned to death."

Suddenly, Monk was absolutely still, but he said nothing.

"Actually, I don't know whether he was burned to death," Crowe amended, "or if he was mercifully killed before the fire got hold."

Crowe was digging a hole for himself. The possibility of murder had never been explored, he was quite sure. And to bring it up now might give Monk the idea that Crowe didn't trust him to do his job.

"Why do you think that?" Monk asked, his face absolutely unreadable.

It was too late to turn back, so he plunged ahead. "Did you consider that the fire might not have been accidental? That it was arson?"

"Of course!" declared Monk. "But we found no proof. And believe me, we looked."

"Would you see it, if it had been skilled enough?"

Crowe did not want to be insulting, but there was no purpose in tiptoeing around the bush.

"That question is its own answer," Monk pointed out. "Are you asking if it was arson so skillfully committed that we couldn't prove it? That question is . . . I don't know how many cases we thought were accidental and turned out to be arson. It certainly happens."

"I don't care about the others, if there are any. You didn't charge anyone in this case. Which tells me that you believed it was accidental. But could it have been arson? The knowledge of that fact would be a powerful weapon with which to blackmail someone."

Monk sat for quite a few seconds, moments ticking by, before he answered, and then it was another question. "And do you believe it was arson? I can't say for sure that it wasn't, only that if it was, it was done by a very clever man and we missed the signs. Why do you want to know, and after all this time?"

"Because I think someone is being blackmailed about it, and I need to know the truth, if I can, before I do anything."

Monk did not ask what he was intending to do, nor did he warn Crowe off any action. "Blackmailed for starting the fire?" he asked instead.

"I don't know," Crowe answered. "But if it truly was

119

an accident, and that is what the police believe, then there would have to have been the kind of proof that convinced you of it."

Monk looked at Crowe for a long time before he finally spoke. "What I believe—and this is off the record, agreed?"

Crowe nodded. "Yes, of course."

Again, a long pause, as if Monk was weighing the wisdom of speaking, or if revealing his thoughts might be unprofessional. Finally, as if having made a decision, he nodded and then spoke. "I suspected that Silas Dolan was behind it, but I couldn't prove it." Before Crowe could respond, he said, "Don't make an enemy of him. He's a hard and clever man, and no one's beaten him yet. And Albert Hollister has more sense than to try. Is that what you wanted me to say?"

"No," Crowe said very softly. "But it is what I was afraid you would say."

Monk drew in breath, and then let it out again. "Be careful, Crowe. You are important to a lot of people. They believe in you, they come to you for help. They trusted you even before you were fully qualified. They paid you with money they didn't have, and they respect you. If you lose that, you won't get it back. And men like Dolan know how to destroy reputations."

Crowe had no answer to these comments. He knew that Monk was right. Their lives were wildly different, but there was something in their natures that was alike. If someone they cared about was in danger, they would fight for them to the end.

"Is it your belief that Hollister and Dolan are responsible for the fire, and very likely the death of the watchman?" Crowe asked.

Something in Monk's face hardened. "Again, off the record: yes, but it's only my opinion. I can't do anything more about it, or believe me, I would." His face was set hard. "And for heaven's sake, Crowe, don't go crusading. Silas Dolan is not only clever, he's dangerous."

Crowe gave a tight smile, then rose slowly to his feet. He turned at the doorway and faced Monk. "Life isn't so tidy, and you know that. Not much point saving my patient's life, only to see her sold into a marriage, and to a monster."

He went out the door, through the anteroom, and then opened the outside door to the wharf and walked back into the cold, dark night.

So, now he knew: Monk had not forgotten, nor had he given up. But he needed solid proof before he could consider reopening the case and making any charges. The question remained: Was the arsonist also the murderer? Was whoever had lit the fire also guilty of Maddock's death?

Crowe was certain that Monk shared his desire to identify the man who had ordered the arson, but if Crowe sprang a trap before he had foolproof evidence, the wrong man might get arrested, and the guilty would remain free, escaping permanently. The gallows were final, and no judge was likely to go back on a verdict he could not undo.

Crowe could well imagine Monk unintentionally making enemies he could not afford, if he were to continue successfully in his job. And that included pursuing a case that nearly everyone considered solved and closed.

Like a lot of things, it was far more complicated than it looked. Crowe knew that it was too early to point a finger. And the last thing he wanted was to sully the reputation of an innocent man. When this happened—and he knew very well that it did—the damage was too often irreversible.

$C$rowe returned to the clinic, and found the warmth a welcome relief. The main room was empty, as if Scuff was finished for the day. But from the other room he heard the click and scrape of a wooden spoon against the rim of the big pot that lived on the stove.

He went into the kitchen. The air was even warmer here, and it closed around him.

"Just about ready," Scuff told him, turning from where he was stirring the pot. "Get washed. And warm up." He hesitated a moment. "Find out anything?" He tried to keep the hope out of his voice, and failed.

Crowe smiled. Scuff was so young. "Learned a little more about Hollister and Silas Dolan," he answered. "An enormous amount of goods were said to have been lost in that fire. Mostly Oriental silks and fine Italian wool, but also furs from Poland and Russia: mink and sable. Even Arctic fox. Very beautiful, very rare, and . . ."

"Very expensive," Scuff finished for him. He pulled the pot off the heat and replaced the lid. It did not fit. It never had, but it kept most of the heat in.

"Very," Crowe agreed. "And various people, dock-workers and the like, remember seeing similar goods around the port after the fire. Not the sort of thing you'd forget. It's something else to swear you saw them, boxes and bales of them, especially the furs. Even a dock-worker knows white fox when he sees it, but there's that risk of revealing what you saw, and making enemies of powerful men." He paused a moment, as if waiting for Scuff to catch up with his thinking. A subtle change in the younger man's face suggested he suddenly realized the implications.

"So, someone swearing that he saw those goods after the fire . . ." Scuff stopped for a moment. "He could be putting his life at risk?"

Crowe nodded. "Right. But that can't stop me from looking into it. I just have to be careful . . . and thorough. Getting specific information is the first step when proving fraud. The challenge isn't proving that those goods were in the warehouse before the fire . . . we know that they were. What we need is proof that those goods were still intact after the fire." He took off his heavy outer coat and sat as near to the stove as he could get.

"The police came today," Scuff said, not looking at Crowe but at the pot on the stove, as if trying to think of something further to do to it. "They asked me several questions." He turned to Crowe. "They asked as if they didn't know who we were, and then they watched when I took a fishhook out of a boy's arm. Had to cut him to get it. Pulling it out would have made a very messy tear. They made a few nasty remarks before that, about what we do here, suggesting that our work with women was in some way immoral. And after that, after I'd removed the hook, they were no less accusing. There were a lot of questions, most of them about you."

Crowe was tired, and he really only wanted to think about the arson, if that's what it was, but he could see that Scuff was upset, and this conversation would be more than their casual catch-up with the day. He leaned into the hard-backed chair and waited.

"I think Hollister sent them," said Scuff. "Or, even more likely, Silas Dolan. They've never bothered us before. They must know perfectly well what we do. And in the world of the River Police, I'm sure they know who my father is." There was a slight self-conscious flush on his cheek. He was still not used to saying "my father" when referring to Monk. He was nothing like Monk to look at, but he could have been Hester's son, with a little imagination.

The burden of his remark caught Crowe's attention. The police had come, and he agreed with Scuff that they were probably sent by Silas Dolan. If Paul Dolan had told his father the truth about the incident with Ellie on the street, he would want to create some kind of a red herring to point the police in another direction.

A wave of coldness went through Crowe, and also a

sense of satisfaction, because it meant that the senior Dolan had something to hide. Otherwise, why send the police to harass him?

Crowe was even more determined to learn if and why Hollister was indebted to Dolan. If he was, and if Hollister was being manipulated by Dolan, the matter would not die. Was Ellie's marriage to Paul Dolan the payoff guaranteeing Hollister's freedom? A man like Silas Dolan would never let the opportunity pass to keep someone under his thumb.

Crowe was quite certain that these policemen had been sent by Dolan as retaliation for his investigation. A warning, perhaps. Or an exercise in power to let Crowe know that the senior Dolan was not a man to be mocked, or in any way taken lightly. Whichever it was, the message was loud and clear.

Crowe understood that he needed help proving his suspicions. A warehouse fire on the river, especially a warehouse with its own wharf, was River Police territory. They were a professional body, so any efforts to cover up the crime had to have been very effective. And Monk had acknowledged that Silas Dolan was clever enough to have left no proof. But even the most intelligent criminals made mistakes. One thing that Monk had not revealed—at least, not in a full-disclosure manner—was whether or not he was still actively in-vestigating the fire.

Crowe thought of his conversation with Monk. The man had been very clear: there had been no proof. And yet Monk shared his view that this had not been a for-tunate accident in which two men had profited.

Crowe watched Scuff add scraps of vegetables to the pot. "Yes, I agree. I think we can assume that Silas Dolan sent the police here. Perhaps it was because I was responsible for his son falling into the gutter."

As soon as he spoke, he pushed that idea away. There had to be more to it than that. Dolan had somehow learned that Crowe was asking questions about the fire. Crowe would be a fool to let his guard down. Foolish . . . and irresponsible.

He shivered. He was still cold inside, because he was hungry. A movement caught his eye. A very small, furry creature was running across the floor, then stopped about five inches from his boot. It was a tiny cat with blue eyes. It looked around, as if judging the distance from where it was, then up to Crowe's lap. It launched itself, landing on his trouser leg, digging its claws in, and then scrambling the rest of the way, until it was curled up in his lap and staring at him.

"What the . . . what is this?" he said to Scuff, after

stifling the word he was about to use. He reached out and touched the kitten's head. It was as smooth as silk. The animal erupted into a loud purring, her little body vibrating with the sound.

"It's a cat," Scuff replied. "A baby cat."

"I can see that!" Crowe said tartly. "I mean what . . . what is it doing here?"

"It's going to catch mice, when it's bigger," Scuff answered, stirring the contents again, quite unnecessarily, as if to avoid meeting Crowe's eyes. "Even the smell of cat keeps most mice away."

"This is not a cat, Scuff. It's not much bigger than most mice, and smaller than a rat!"

Scuff dropped the spoon and stared at him in alarm.

Crowe's pity was instant. "Don't look like that! There are no rats that size here! And you're right, the smell of cats keeps most rodents away. Where did you get it? The little thing's scarcely weaned!"

Scuff stood frozen for a moment, then took a deep breath. "She's a present. A payment, if you like."

"For what? Why on earth did you accept it?" And then something captured his attention. He turned. It was a child, around five years old, possibly, and she was looking at him with apprehension, eyes wide.

"Mattie?" he said.

"I brung her for you. To pay you for stitching me up."

"You don't need to pay—" Crowe began.

"Yes, she did," Scuff interrupted, coming away from the stove and picking the little creature off Crowe's lap, putting it on his own shoulder, and then gently stroking it with one finger. "This is Rosie. She's Mattie's best friend, but she gave her to us. And you don't need to worry about looking after her, because Mattie will do that." He stared very steadily at Crowe. "All we need to do is have enough milk. I don't know what else she eats, but Mattie does." He swallowed. "She'll look after her. And the cat will catch mice when she's bigger. She'll know how to do that herself."

"It's a she?" Crowe asked. "How do you know? Did you look?" The creature was so small, and with thick fur, that this seemed unlikely.

"Mattie says that she can tell by the color of the kitten," Scuff said with authority, but Crowe could tell from his face that he had no idea himself.

Crowe turned to Mattie.

She nodded vigorously. "And all the ginger striped ones are boys. Or nearly all. Girl cats are better at catching mouses."

"Are they. And where is she going to sleep, so she's safe?"

Mattie turned round and pointed to the blanket on the floor in the corner, with a pillow lying on it. "With me. I will look after her." She seemed to run out of courage. And words.

"I see," Crowe said slowly. "Thank you. You must tell me if you are not comfortable there. Will you do that?"

She nodded slowly.

"Good. Have you had supper?"

She looked at him, confused.

"Something to eat," he explained. She shook her head. He looked at the kitten, now asleep on Scuff's shoulder. "And her."

"Rosie," Mattie reminded him.

"Rosie. Yes, well, you look after her. Keep her clean, do you understand me?"

She nodded, then her face broke into a wide smile. Scuff was right. She still had all her milk teeth. How on earth were they going to look after this child?

Scuff reached up and unfastened Rosie's claws from his jersey and handed her back to Mattie. Then he got down three dishes and a saucer. He served three equal-sized portions of stew into the bowls, and a very small amount into the saucer. Then he put the three bowls on the table, and Rosie and the saucer on the floor. "Dinner is served," he said.

*I*t was a bitterly cold night, but the fire was always lit in the winter and the warmth remained in the iron of the stove long after the coals were burned to no more than embers.

Crowe was having a restless sleep. Dark dreams kept waking him up: surging swells of water he couldn't outrun; fire burning around him, with no way out. He finally got out of bed and wandered into the kitchen for a drink of water. According to the clock on the sideboard, it was nearly three thirty.

He riddled some of the ash through and put more coals on the fire. Now it would last until morning. Something stirred in the corner, and he felt his hair stand on end, until he remembered the child. Perhaps she should not have to sleep in the kitchen? Should he ask Scuff if she could sleep in a corner of his room? But she would be cold!

He walked over quietly, his stockinged feet soundless on the stone floor with its patchy pieces of old carpet. Mattie was curled up inside the blanket, and sound asleep, her face completely untroubled, the tiny kitten nestled under her chin.

Crowe had no emotional ties; he was used to being completely free. He was responsible for doing his job well, but so was everyone. He often thought back to those days when he had accepted help from Hester Monk and, with her support, had attained the professional qualifications that had been his dream for as long as he could remember. His gratitude was intense, and he was glad to find a way to show it by helping Scuff. It was a responsibility, he knew, but he had done it for Hester, who had deserved this, and more.

Helping Scuff carried its own rewards. The boy learned quickly, and he always went the extra mile and did many things without being asked. It had not taken long for Crowe to become accustomed to having him around. Like Crowe, Scuff understood about hunger and cold, loneliness and gratitude. Crowe would miss him, were he to leave.

But he had not foreseen this child! And a girl! He knew nothing about girls, except medically, of course. While he was certainly a man with feelings, opinions, humor, he had no idea about the emotional needs of a child. He had always liked animals, and was happy to treat them when they were ill or injured. But this kitten presented much less of a problem than the child! In six months or less, the cat would be independent. But the child? She was a completely different matter. It could be a decade before she was able to make her own way, and even that was young. What should he teach her? What could he?

His feet were cold, standing on the stone floor. The blanket covering Mattie had fallen sideways. If she moved even a little, it would slip off. He bent and tucked it in. The cat—Rosie, she had called it—gave a sigh and a slight purr, then went back to sleep.

Crowe straightened up and walked over to the counter, where he poured himself a small glass of water, carried it back to his room, and crawled into his bed.

None of what concerned him needed to be settled tonight. In the morning, he would begin again, to find out one way or the other, and for certain, if the warehouse fire had been arson or an accident. The whole issue of Hollister's debt to Silas Dolan had to rest on that, didn't it? Ellie was going to marry Paul Dolan for some reason other than love. Yet again, Crowe was plagued by the certainty that she loathed him. And perhaps feared him as well. From the moment he had seen them standing together under that lamp, and Dolan had slapped her, her feelings toward him had been terribly clear.

Crowe was running out of time. With Christmas approaching, he needed to find the answer, and solid proof of it. Silas Dolan was going to arrange his son's wedding as soon as the seasonal celebrations were over.

What if Crowe could prove that the fire was arson? That didn't make either of the Dolans guilty. They had enemies, and one or more of them might have been responsible for the fire. Or it might have been accidental, perhaps from someone being careless. But would learning the answer to this be any use for Ellie? Yes! If it had been an accident, or the fire started by an enemy of the Dolans, then this might release Ellie from the obligation to protect her father by marrying Paul Dolan. Crowe had to admit to himself that this was his primary goal.

He pushed the thought away. Dolan was guilty of *something*, he was certain, and Hollister was, at the least, complicit.

*C*rowe got up early and woke Scuff. He needed to tell him what he was going to do, and when he would be back.

Scuff woke up slowly, blinking in the lamplight filtering into a room that was still dark.

"Sorry," Crowe began. "From what you said, Silas Dolan is after us. We need to know more, and I'm going to look for it. There's plenty of oatmeal. Get yourself breakfast, and Mattie, too. And be sure to keep enough milk to feed the cat."

Crowe stood up and began to say goodbye, and then realized that Scuff was asleep again. "Good night," he said quietly.

Crowe reminded himself yet again that he did not approve of collecting old debts—or any debts, for that matter—but he needed information, and quickly. There were several people he could try. It would be less trouble to start with those who were easy to find and willing to talk, and go after others only if necessary. He could not afford to lose any time. He already knew the people who would be most willing to speak to him.

He thought of starting with the men who worked on the barges. But they were a tight-knit group, and it was not so easy to pull information from them. No, he would start with several firemen. After he had learned more about the fire, and collected information that could be important, then he would talk to the police.

Stepping into the cold of morning, he decided there were several questions he had to ask. Of the firemen he knew, who would provide the most information? And if someone actually had moved Dolan's goods before the fire, how had they done it? Or did it matter? Crowe needed to know, to fully understand, step by step, how all of this had been done.

Moving the goods was done by water, that was certain. The river was on the warehouse's doorstep. No noisy engines to be overheard. Silently, and on the tide. He had spent enough time near the river to know the strength of the tide and the currents. It was not so difficult to wait for the turn of the tide, then load the goods—that would be quick and quiet—and then go up-river with the surge of tidal water. The goods would be miles away before anyone was aware of it.

The first thing was to check the tides on the night of the fire. When did they turn? When could one go up-river on the flood tide? Or get barges to carry the full cargo beyond where they would be looked for? The cargo would be unloaded at that point, wouldn't it? Or moored somewhere discreetly, and then carried upriver with the next flood tide.

These were a few of the things he needed to look into. Until he knew the truth, he would not be sure if any of his theories were viable. If the fire was indeed arson, then Silas Dolan had had the fabrics removed either the night before the fire, or earlier on the night when the fire took place. It had to be when it was dark and there were no witnesses. Which meant that someone, or several, had done the work. But who?

Crowe reminded himself that the worst possible result was to learn that the Dolans had got out of it somehow, possibly by blaming Hollister for both the fire and the death of Maddock. And then it might follow that this Maddock might also be guilty of the theft of the goods. If he was in the warehouse, he must have seen, or been part of, loading goods onto the barge. But perhaps he was an innocent man, and his witnessing this was the reason for his death.

Was everything Hollister's fault, or had it been made to look as though it were? Crowe had considered this before, and it seemed to make more sense that Dolan had duped Hollister. Crowe warned himself away from wishful thinking. He wanted Dolan to be guilty, and Hollister not. But Dolan was clever, and more than capable of placing the guilt wholly on Hollister. Was he threatening to do this? Was this why Hollister was trapped, and it was Ellie who was going to pay the price?

Crowe wanted to free Ellie from this prison, and he hoped that this would include a way out for her father.

Once he knew the truth, he could see what the possibilities were. Which is why identifying the tides was so important.

As for the barges, had they arrived at the dock one by one? Or had they come together, connected in a string, which meant they could be managed by only two men? The latter seemed to be the better choice. A string of barges, yes. But after all this time, how could he prove or disprove it?

Crowe had already found information at the library: newspaper accounts providing the date of the fire and the amount of damage. Through this, he had been able to figure out an estimate of the cost of the goods destroyed. He had also learned how many fire engines had attended the fire, and how long the blaze had burned. But there was more he needed, information that might complete the picture for him. What day of the week had the fire taken place? He still had to confirm the tide times and the weather. Tides were predictable to the minute, as was the moon. The weather was not.

Was there any other variable that had to be considered?

"Why am I putting myself through this?" he murmured as he crossed the road. The answer came quickly. It probably didn't matter so much how many barges were used, or where the goods were hidden. All that really mattered was who had planned the fraud . . . and who was responsible for a man's death. But this wasn't enough for Crowe. He was a doctor, trained to look at every possibility. Partial information, even if it brought him to the answers he sought, was not enough. He wanted to know more. He needed to know . . . all.

On his list was the availability of the barges needed to move all the valuable cargo from the warehouse. It would take a skilled bargee with a lifetime of experience to guide heavily loaded barges upriver. Only an expert would know how to take advantage of all the tides, understand the eddies, sandbanks, and so on.

If he could find this man, then the tide, or even the precise time of the fire, no longer mattered.

Crowe shifted his mind to the barges. He was quite certain a whole bunch of them had been needed to move the entire cargo. Wool was very bulky stuff, even when it was spun and woven into fine cloth. A bolt of silk was heavy. Furs had to be packed and boxed carefully, and they, too, were very bulky. What he knew was that it was a large shipment, but that its value paled next to the loss of a man's life.

He made a list in his head of the people he knew who were best experienced to help him with the answers. It took the rest of the day, carefully questioning them all, before he began to feel he was making progress. His queries were designed to learn what he needed, but without being so direct that these people would wonder why he wanted to know such things. Or feel threatened by his questions.

$\mathcal{B}$y seven o'clock that evening, after almost three hours of working in the dark, Crowe was finally satisfied that he had all he needed to know. Along the way, he had even learned one or two additional facts. They were like grace notes in a piece of music.

He went into a pub, took a seat by the fire, and went over all that he had learned.

On the evening of the fire, which was estimated to have started around midnight, the flood tide had begun a little after five, and was slack for a good quarter hour before that. Which meant that, as it had been early February, it was dark by then. That gave the men involved less than half an hour of slack water, just after dark, in which to move goods from the warehouse, with its own wharf, onto the barges.

The location of Hollister's wharf was ideal. Crowe

wondered if Hollister had thought to have men working after dark for several evenings before the fire, in order to forestall any suspicion.

As for loading the goods onto the barges, they were probably able to accomplish that with the help of a relatively small derrick, and in less than an hour.

By the time the tide was fully turned and flooding upstream, the loaded barges would have been out on the water. And by midnight, when the fire was started, they would have been several miles away.

*I*t was late when Crowe got home. From outside, the clinic looked dark . . . and silent. The entrance was so familiar that he did not need to see in order to use his key to open the door.

He closed it behind him and pushed the bolts home, and then stood in the darkness and the warmth for a minute, feeling the safety wrap around him. The fire must have been banked up and closed, for it to still be smoldering. He must remember to thank Scuff for that, and also ask him to check their fuel supplies.

His eyes were quickly used to the dark; there were

very few streetlamps in this area. He could see the out-
line of the blankets on the floor in the corner, and the
hump in the middle that would be the child. He walked
over and looked down at her. Someone had tucked her
in. Scuff? Of course, there was no one else, and the kitten was tucked in, too.

He stayed there for a moment. He had a sense of
being home. And now he had a new responsibility. The
child must always be fed, and kept warm and safe, noticed, and talked to. And one day someone would have
to teach her to read, write, and count. That would be
another job for Scuff!

Crowe took off his boots so his footsteps into his bed-
room would be silent. He had a whole night in which to
plan his next step.

*C*rowe was up, dressed, and out early the following
morning. His findings of the previous day confirmed
much of what he had already learned. He feared it
would take an army of detectives to trace any of the
goods claimed on the insurance for the warehouse fire,
and then prove they were deliberately moved out of the

142

warehouse before the fire was started. That was a major charge, the starting of a fire, but it paled against the element of murder.

Crowe began by questioning the owners of barges, men he knew, and hoped he could trust.

Further up the river, he met with a lock keeper. He wanted to determine if the goods had gone further inland than this first set of locks. The man, who was reluctant to talk, assured him that they had not.

Nevertheless, he went even further inland, where the gatekeeper of the second lock spoke without even consulting his logs.

"No one carrying such a cargo passed through here," the man told Crowe.

"Who could handle such a load?" he asked. "Also, who would be the best at moving it quickly and secretly?"

Again, there were no answers.

Crowe was able to find a few men who slept in the open, meaning they often saw things others did not, but there was no information to be had, other than occasional observations.

However, between the lock keepers and assorted men who might have witnessed something—and declared they had not—he heard varied stories. Taking notes, he began to see cross-references, helping him to pin down what was most likely to be the truth. With these bits of information now in hand, would it be worth speaking to Hollister directly? He had to try.

$C$rowe walked up the hill toward the house of Albert Hollister. It was after six, already pitch-dark and the road iced over, especially where it had been recently re-surfaced and flattened. He tried to avoid those repaired areas, since the old, rough surfaces were easier to navigate. The new, slick surfaces might make for a smoother carriage ride, but they wreaked havoc with one's balance when trying to walk on an icy night. There was a kind of bitter humor in that.

He knocked on the back door, hoping that Barker, the butler, would remember him and allow him in.

He had practiced all the way up the hill exactly what he would say, and had come to a conclusion he was satisfied with. Even so, he hesitated on the doorstep. When no one answered his knock, he rang the bell.

It was not Barker who answered, but a boot boy, who stared up at Crowe with curiosity.

A decision was required immediately. "May I speak to Mr. Barker, please?" Crowe asked.

"Yes, sir." The boy gulped. "Who shall I say is calling?"

A gust of wind came like an icy breath out of the dark, brushing past Crowe and into the kitchen.

"Billy!" came a sharp voice from inside the kitchen, a woman's voice.

"Yes, ma'am." The boy took a deep breath. "Would you like to come in, sir? I need to close the door; Cook is getting cold."

Crowe hid a smile and followed the boy into a large, warm kitchen. It seemed that the entire household staff was there, eight or nine people in all.

Crowe's heart sank. This was the home Ellie was accustomed to. If she dropped a handkerchief, there would be someone near to pick it up for her. There was nothing for Crowe to hope for, except to save her, the one thing she could not do for herself. But he could not save her father if the man had contrived to defraud and had caused Maddock's death in the process. Please God, he had been coerced into his part in it, rather than had chosen it!

He must explain himself.

"I would like to speak to Mr. Hollister, please. It is a business matter of some urgency."

Barker rose to his feet. "May I tell him what it is regarding, sir, before I ask him to interrupt his evening? No one is hurt, I hope."

"No one that I am aware of," Crowe replied. "I would like to keep it that way."

The message was not lost on Barker. Without speaking further, the man turned and went out of the room. He did not ask Crowe's name. Had he remembered it?

Crowe was left standing.

Barker returned and conducted Crowe through to the withdrawing room, where Hollister was standing. He was wearing a red velvet-collared smoking jacket, and the light shone on the surfaces of it as he moved. Hollister waited until Barker had left and then closed the door before he spoke.

"Good evening, Doctor. What can I do for you?" His tone was more polite than it had been that last meeting, as if he was now remembering his debt to Crowe for saving Ellie's life. He had given a small amount of money to the clinic, although he was certainly aware that the sum was hardly compensation for the care she had received. Had he sought the services of his own private doctor, he would have paid him ten times as much. And, Crowe assumed, he would have paid it gladly.

Crowe stood there, still not certain what he wanted to say. He did not want to sound so proper as to make the words meaningless. And he certainly did not wish to make more of an enemy of the man than he already had. He was confident that the police, when given what he knew, would reopen the investigation into the distribution of the goods Hollister and Dolan had claimed were burned in the warehouse fire, a fire that Hollister had later claimed as a major loss with his insurance company.

"Good evening, Mr. Hollister," Crowe replied. "I work on the waterfront, as you know. I serve many people who work on the river." The moment he spoke, he saw a scowl appear on Hollister's face.

"I am aware of that. Please come to the point."

Crowe took a deep breath. The time had arrived. "Mr. Hollister, have you thought of the consequences of the police tracing certain barges up the river immediately after the fire in your warehouse?"

It wasn't the truth, at least not yet, but he needed to nudge this man into conversation.

"Now?" Hollister said with disbelief. At the same time, he seemed far from concerned. "For heaven's sake, man, that's ancient history! It was investigated at the time. There's nothing more to look at. It has, quite literally, gone up in smoke." Suddenly his face froze. "What are you really here for?"

There was a knock on the door, and almost immediately Ellie came in. Paul Dolan was on her heels. He scowled at Crowe.

She was wearing an evening gown of gray and silver. It held no real color, and yet it glowed, and her face was haloed by the brightness of her hair, pale gold, like a light. And around her shoulders was the rich, luxuriously thick gleam of a white stole of Arctic fox fur.

"You look beautiful, my dear," Hollister said, breaking the prickly silence.

"Paul gave it to me," she said, her voice wobbling a little as she touched the fur. "An early Christmas present." She glanced at Crowe for a second, or even less— nodded in acknowledgment of his presence—then back at her father. Her voice wobbled again when she spoke. "We're leaving now, Father. I won't be late. It's going to be very cold, and Paul says the roads are iced already."

Hollister seemed to have difficulty finding his voice. "Dr. Crowe was just leaving."

Crowe inclined his head toward Ellie, and then turned and left. As he moved cautiously along the icy road, he saw only Ellie's pale, slender shoulders, and that Arctic fox wrapped around them.

*W*hen Scuff awoke, Crowe was already gone. His first thought was to make breakfast for Mattie, and he supposed Rosie as well. What did baby cats eat for breakfast?

He made scrambled eggs on toast for himself and Mattie. He needed only one glance at her face to see that it was very welcome. When he came back from boiling the water and filling the teapot, the kitten was on the floor. She was standing next to her own saucer, which held a little piece of toast, over-buttered, and a spoonful of Mattie's egg.

Mattie looked up at Scuff anxiously.

He smiled at her.

Her face lit with pleasure and she smiled back. They both looked at Rosie, who was ignoring them and gobbling up the scrambled egg.

Scuff had several patients to see, nothing serious. Sometimes, they came in with a case of anxiety. If he assured them that a wound was healing, or that some ache or pain was of no concern, they went away happy.

This morning, a woman came simply to offer a freshly baked loaf of bread, still warm from the oven.

149

"Thank you very much," Scuff said with sincerity.

"Thank you very much," said Mattie, echoing both his words and his tone. She stood so close to him that he felt her weight against his leg.

When the same police sergeant and constable as before came later in the morning, Rosie was curled up and asleep on the blanket, and Mattie had taken the broom and the dustpan and was busy doing something in one of the other rooms.

Scuff had just opened his books, taking this lull as a chance to study, when the outside door swung open and the policemen walked in.

"Not busy, Doctor?" the sergeant asked, his tone unmistakably sarcastic. He knew that Scuff wasn't a doctor. At least, not yet, which made his comment seem all the more satisfying to himself.

Scuff's instinctive thought was to explain that he was reading, and to question the sergeant as to whether he could read. He could even offer him the book, with all its long medical terminology. But he let the comment pass. He could not afford to make an enemy of the man. It wasn't that he was feeling vulnerable, but he had to look out for Mattie. "A few patients expected, but I'm using what free time I have to study," he replied. "Can I help you, Sergeant?"

The man did not have a ready response.

Scuff assumed that the idea of study was outside his experience. He waited, trying to look innocent. He was well practiced at it, although it was a long time since he had needed this skill.

"You've been around asking questions," the sergeant said abruptly. "Poking into things what's none of your business."

"No," Scuff said honestly. "I haven't left the clinic." He did not add to it. Doing so would make him sound nervous. He noticed when other people did that. Too much explanation was a sign of tension, guilt, the need to misdirect. He waited, looking back at the sergeant.

"You been asking about the fire in February," the sergeant said, as if accusing Scuff of something illegal.

The constable stood beside him, looking nervous.

"No, I have not," Scuff repeated, again without elaborating.

The sergeant was growing irritated. "You'd be a lot cleverer if you was to mind your own business. We could shut this place down, you know."

Scuff remained quiet.

"Just warning you," the sergeant said grimly. "You become a nuisance and you'll pay." He gave a smile, but it was more a baring of the teeth. Then he turned on his heel and went out, closely followed by the constable, who had said nothing at all, and looked unhappy.

Scuff was still wondering what he should do about the police warning when Mattie pushed open the door to the kitchen and stood just inside it. She looked very frightened, biting her lip. "What are we going to do?"

Scuff felt the weight of her fear as if it were a physical thing. There was only one thing he could think of. "I'm going to speak to some of the people I used to know, when I was younger." He wondered how else he could help Crowe wade through all of this. It was the least he could do for the man who had given him such a promising future.

Mattie looked lost; her eyes were wide with concern.

"I won't be long," he told her. "Just going to talk to some people on the river. Do you know what a mudlark is?"

"'Course I do!"

"Well, that's what I used to be. When I was your age, and older."

The disbelief in her eyes needed no words.

"You don't believe me? I was. Then Mr. Monk looked after me. Gave me a home. Taught me how to read and write."

There was hope in her eyes, so fragile it would shatter at the slightest clumsy touch. "Are you looking after me?" she said at last.

"Yes." He made it a definite statement. Maybe it was a foolish thing to say, but there was no alternative. "Dr. Crowe, too. And you will look after Rosie. I know she's a cat, but she needs looking after as well." He took a breath. "So, I'm going to go and speak to some of the people I used to know." She nodded solemnly, as if she didn't know what he wanted, so she couldn't say she would do it.

"Stay here, Mattie. I'll lock the door when I go, and you don't open it to anyone. Promise me?"

"I promise," she said, her face solemn.

"And look after Rosie, but don't let her out. I'll come back as soon as I can. And Dr. Crowe will, too. We both have keys. And don't touch the stove. In fact, don't go near it. It's stoked to last all day. If you're hungry, there are some cold potatoes in the larder. You can eat them all, if you want to."

"Can I?"

"Yes. And pour a little milk out for Rosie."

As he walked out of the clinic, he felt sadness moving through him. Christmas was nearly here. He promised himself to return with even the smallest toy, and perhaps something for Rosie, too.

Mattie deserved to feel the joy of Christmas Day. And to have a place she could call home.

*I*t was bitterly cold closer to the water. Scuff knew what it felt like to be outside in this. He had not yet forgotten, and perhaps he never would. At first, it had felt very strange to sleep in a bed, with blankets and warmth. It was good, but strangely uncomfortable, until he had become used to it. He wondered if Mattie shared this feeling.

Before leaving the clinic, he had taken some money from the drawer where it was kept. He bought out all the ham sandwiches from one of the peddlers on the road, and carried them down to a large waterfront loading dock. He still knew the best places to shelter. Memory of cold returned easily: the wind that found every crack in your clothing, as if it had rearranged the garments with fingers as cold as ice. He forgot it most of the time. But here on the water's edge, with the wind whining through the cranes' tall skeletons, and around the odd bales that had been left, and behind everything that could double as shelter, memory came back.

He didn't know any of the mudlarks he saw along the shore, but, once, he must have looked just like them: thin and cold. And he knew where to find them. He also knew that they were invisible to most people, meaning they could witness events without being noticed. The police treated them like criminals, but Scuff knew better. These children cared only about survival.

Today, he was less concerned about getting information than he was about Crowe being upset with him for helping. But Scuff could help! He knew these boys, how they lived and thought, and how to quickly earn their trust. And what if Crowe did get angry? Scuff pushed that thought away. He would do anything to help Crowe.

"Want half my sandwich?" he offered one boy, perhaps a little older than the two he could see in the shadows.

The boy looked about ten, which meant he was probably more like twelve. Hunger did this to a child. The boy held out his hand. Scuff looked at him closely. He knew he would incur respect, not resentment, if he offered a bargain. "Trade you?"

"Got nothing," the boy said sharply, disappointment in his face.

Other boys moved slowly toward him, suspicion marked in their narrowed eyes.

"What're you lookin' for?" asked one of them.

"Information," Scuff replied.

The boy's expression tightened.

Scuff knew he was taking a risk, going against his orders from the police to stay away from this case, and Crowe's orders to stay in the clinic and fill in for him. But how could Scuff not do this? "About barges and cargoes," he said. "And last February, when that big fire happened. One of you will have seen something. Let me know, and then we'll all have sandwiches. And I want the truth." He smiled as he said it. Waves of memory washed over him: the lack of physical things, the way the cold wrapped around him, freezing his flesh.

He drew in his breath and let it out slowly. "Tell me, what did you see the night of the fire?" As he was speaking, he was unpacking the sandwiches and passing them into eager, grubby hands.

Nobody waited to be told to eat, and Scuff knew to be patient.

He waited until they were finished, only a matter of minutes, then he began the questions.

At first, the answers were slow, as if wading into deep water, but soon the boys understood exactly what it was he wanted to know. It was what Scuff needed, but he was concerned that their gratitude, and perhaps their hunger for more food, would prompt answers that were not accurate. He questioned them as much as he could without making them think he doubted them.

"How could you see that?" he asked, after a particularly vivid account. He looked at the boy's innocent, unlined face, smeared with dirt. It became anxious; he was only a few years older than Mattie.

"They got lights then, don't they? Not bright, like, but enough to see where they're going."

"And be able to see everyone else?" Scuff pointed out.

"Misty night, weren't it." That was not a question, only the boy's way of stating the fact.

"Full moon?" Scuff asked. He already knew that it was the day after a full moon, so there could have been light in the sky.

"Close to one," the boy agreed. "Cold and, on and off, raining a bit."

"So why were you outside?" Scuff tried to keep his voice reflecting interest, not criticism or disbelief.

"Wanted to see what they was doing, didn't I."

"And what were they doing?"

"Loading a whole lot of stuff out of the warehouse and putting it on barges."

"How many barges? Do you know?"

The boy put up his fingers one by one. "That many," he replied, indicating seven.

"Were they loaded full?" Scuff asked. He looked at the other boys who had said they were there. They all nodded. "And where did they go? Upriver or down?" He saw the discomfort in their faces, even boredom, but he needed to be sure they understood his questions and gave consistent answers.

"Up," they all said, nodding their heads.

"How far up?" He knew they could not know the answer to that. Would they invent something, to please him?

"Dunno," they said one by one. They looked unhappy that they could not give him more.

"Thank you," he said. "You have helped a lot. Maybe I'll have money by Christmas, and we'll have another ham sandwich. But I gotta go back to work now. If any of you get hurt or sick, come to the clinic. I owe you."

They looked at each other, then back at him. And then, slowly, each one of them smiled.

*O*n the way back to the clinic, Scuff passed a street vendor selling little hand-knitted dolls. He dug into his pocket and pulled out some coins from the clinic's reserve. They could go another few days without some supplies, although he wasn't sure what. When he tucked the doll into his pocket and thought of Mattie's smile when she saw it, he felt a warmth run through him.

He returned to the clinic, where Mattie was overjoyed to see him, and set about his duties.

Sometime later, Crowe returned. Scuff hoped his mentor would be pleased, and not angry, by what he had learned.

"Let's hear it," Crowe said, as if reserving judgment until the goods were delivered.

"It's all from the mudlarks," he said, and then rushed ahead to tell Crowe everything he had learned, more or less in their own words.

As he spoke, Crowe's face changed from stern to hopeful. "This is exactly what I've wanted to hear," he said. "And, in some ways, dreaded."

Crowe explained that he had already checked the weather and tides, as well as the fullness of the moon. "The boys might lie, if they believed it would be in their interest, but I doubt they'd tell exactly the same lie, and with the same details."

"You sound as if you don't quite believe them," said Scuff.

Crowe shook his head. "No, I think they're telling the

truth. It's just that, in the back of my mind, I had hoped that Hollister was not involved."

Scuff understood his disappointment, but there was no way Hollister would not have been aware of the removal of the goods from his own warehouse. And both Hollister and Dolan had collected insurance money for their losses.

There was the added element of the River Police having checked for arson. While they suspected that the fire might have been intentionally set, there was no proof.

*C*rowe took some time to think about everything Scuff had told him. He knew that both Hollister and Dolan had enemies. Rich and successful men usually did, even if the animosity was based on nothing more than envy. Was it too much to hope that one of these enemies had planned it all, hoping to stain the reputations of Hollister and Dolan? Neither man had taken kindly to the suspicions that had followed naturally from the event, and then its subsequent investigation. At the same time, no one had been blamed. Crowe believed that, even if someone knew the truth, a wise man who wanted to continue in business, or stay alive, did not make accusations against someone like Silas Dolan.

He was also certain that it didn't really matter what he believed. He had to find the evidence—hard evidence—that Dolan's goods had been taken upriver. And not by some nefarious third party, but by Dolan's own people.

The words of a group of riverbank urchins were worth nothing at all to men like Dolan. Crowe believed them, but did it matter? If faced with the mudlarks' information, Dolan would say that, for a ham sandwich, these boys would swear they had seen Santa Claus riding across the sky on a golden sled drawn by reindeer. Or even unicorns, for that matter.

With a chill running through him, Crowe remembered his visit to Hollister, and how Ellie had come into the withdrawing room wearing that Arctic fox stole. The same kind of rare and luxurious fur as had been supposedly lost in the warehouse fire.

He had seen from the look in her eyes that she did not like it. Was that because she believed the cost—the lives of animals—was too high? Or was it because she feared that it was part of the cargo that had been reported as destroyed?

Had she come in wearing that stole so that he would see it? And recognize it? Or had Paul given it to her knowing that her father would recognize it? It could not be the former, because she'd had no way of knowing that Crowe would be in that room. Unless, of course, Barker had told her. Was she wearing it as a warning to Crowe . . . or to her father? Had Paul draped it over her shoulders to mock her father?

Hollister had to know where it came from, whether Ellie realized it or not. How could he find out? It pained him to think that she might have even the smallest idea that the fire was arson. Or that the night watchman's—Maddock's—death was murder. The fur could be evidence of both.

It pained him even more to think she was trapped in a betrothal to a man he was sure she loathed, an arrangement that very soon would become a marriage. Uglier than that, and more profoundly distressing, was that she might have worn that stole because she understood precisely what it represented, and who the culprits were. She could be warning Crowe not to pursue it, because of what it would cost her.

He shook off this thought as unfair. He was being tortured by his fears, and solving nothing. He needed to face the truth, whatever it was.

His primary goal was to find out if he could trace any of the goods to the same destination on the river. Merchants still had bills of lading, and records of large payments for such loads of goods, even if they were bought by several people. The backwash of such huge deals did not simply disappear.

There was no need to explain to Scuff where he was going this time, or why. Scuff was the one who had uncovered the vital information, and Crowe understood that he had done this out of loyalty.

He made a brief journey to buy supplies the clinic needed. Mostly, it was a matter of bandages, and surgical spirits to make things clean.

When he returned, he spoke briefly to Scuff. He could not avoid speaking with Mattie, and to the little cat, too. He picked Rosie up with one hand, and set her more or less on his shoulder, where she immediately began to purr loudly, and knead her claws into the fabric of his jacket.

Mattie giggled, and her eyes were wide with pleasure.

He told her where he was going, but not why, and that he wanted her to look after the kitten, and to help Scuff by doing all the cleaning up he asked her to.

"Yes, I will," she said with the utmost solemnity.

He left satisfied, feeling that he had exited his true home, a place where he belonged, where he was expected and needed. In spite of the importance of this errand, and the difficulty of it, he knew he needed to look for the one bargee who might help him.

It surprised him that Mac hadn't come to mind sooner. Perhaps his concerns for Ellie, and an infatuation that he was finding difficult to acknowledge, were interfering with his normally logical mind!

It was nearly ten in the morning when he found Mac, and much further upriver than expected. The man was guiding a whole string of heavily loaded barges, at least seven or eight. Crowe knew too well how hard this work was, but years of practice had perfected Mac's instincts. Although it required considerable strength, anyone watching would see a man moving with grace and perfect balance.

Crowe followed Mac's instructions to sit on a pile of cargo on the first barge, and to remain there until he was told otherwise. This would give Crowe time to re-weigh and consider the information he had found. Part of this was Scuff's confirmation that a very large cargo had been removed from Hollister's wharf just before the fire, even as many as seven barges, all of them needed to carry the entire cargo of "lost items" upstream. From there, everything seemed to have disappeared. Which was, of course, impossible.

Crowe tried to think it through. He was certain that there were only a number of places that could deal in such fine fabrics as silk and Italian wool. And, as it happened, furs. These were all considered luxury goods in the extreme, so it would require a company with wide distribution to sell them. But it would also require large containers for storing the goods. That is, until they could be sold and moved.

He wondered what he needed to begin his search for tracing Dolan's shipment. Seated on the barge, he watched the banks slip past as Mac steered their way upstream.

They passed small islets in the river, bare trees with their branches stretching up, as if they were holding up the sky. The wind caused little ripples on the open water. Crowe thought of other voyages he had made years ago, as a ship's surgeon. He had seen marvelous places then. So much time had passed, yet these images continued to enrich his imagination. Perhaps he would tell Mattie about them one day.

They passed many wharfs, but smaller than those in London, which were among the busiest in the world. The cargo could have been deposited anywhere along these miles of waterways, except that the barges from the main port would be like the one he was on: large, heavy, and long. Even the most skilled bargee could turn a barge only within a certain minimum length of water.

"Hey, Mac!" he said on sudden impulse. "You awake?"

The bargee turned around and smiled. "Gonna finally tell me?"

"Tell you what?" Crowe asked carefully.

"What you're really after."

"You think . . ."

"I do," Mac agreed. "Perhaps I can help, if I know what on earth you're looking for."

"A shipment of luxury fur and fabrics that someone was killed for. I need to know if they could have been moved before a fire. And if so, where they were moved to."

"Killed? A friend of yours?" Mac asked.

"No, but a friend of mine could be next."

Mac stared at him for a while, studying his eyes. Crowe did not blink. The silence was easy. He had known Mac for years, on and off. They had even shared food and warmth in those days when Crowe had so little. Crowe had once treated him medically, but that was nearly twenty years ago. Mac had never let him down. Or, more importantly, Mac had never let anyone down.

"Ah," Mac said slowly. "Crusading again, are we?" He

turned back to his pole and the long sweep of the next stroke. "We'll try at Murphy's wharf. Know a few people there."

Crowe nodded. What friends did Hollister have as far up the river as this? Or perhaps more importantly, what friends did Dolan have?

Crowe knew that Mac was prepared to chase all possibilities. He was like a dog on a scent. They shared that.

With Mac in the lead, they moved from one location to another. Crowe left the questions to his old friend, who was known and respected up and down the river.

Their efforts proved to be well worth it, and what they discovered took them both by surprise. They were able to trace a huge shipment, seven barges in all, carrying goods that were moved in the dark. Mac's friend remembered that none of the cargo could be allowed to get wet.

"River water's dirty," said the man, eyes darting around to be sure he wasn't heard. "Not sure, but might have been wool and silk. Expensive stuff, y'know? Stowed in the nearest of those warehouses."

Crowe knew that these fabrics would quickly rot if soiled, unless thoroughly washed and dried out. Hardly a thing someone could do discreetly.

"I'm guessing there couldn't be two such shipments like that in one month," said Mac, after the man had scurried away.

Crowe said nothing. He was now certain that this was the transfer of goods orchestrated by Dolan and abetted by Hollister.

*C*rowe returned from upriver and arrived at the clinic a little before midnight. He was relieved to see a light inside; he wanted to share everything he had learned with Scuff.

They sat by the stove, which was still radiating heat throughout the room. Mattie was sound asleep, wrapped in her blanket in the far corner, with Rosie curled up against her.

The men spoke quietly, so as not to disturb her, and because they did not want her to get half the thread of the story, and then worry about the other half.

"You sure?" Scuff said quietly. The moment the words were out, he wished he had not asked. Neither of them wanted Hollister to be guilty, and yet it was the only answer that made sense. The missing goods had not surfaced anywhere near Hollister's warehouse, or its ruins. And surely the River Police would have found them within a couple of weeks if they had remained nearby. A river man, especially a bargee, knew exactly how far a flood tide would carry them, and could calculate within five or ten minutes how long it would take to unload such a cargo.

But unload onto what? A wharf, and then another warehouse? A train that could handle the whole shipment and get it inland before dawn? He did not yet know, but he had heard enough to be certain that it had happened. The Thames River Police would match up the details when he gave them the information, and the names of those who were prepared to swear to it. He hoped that Mac had the sense not to ask too many questions. Arson was a crime of a different, more serious order, not so much for the insurance companies, although this certainly mattered, but because fire in a warehouse was the key to this entire business. And a death. Which meant that where there was arson, there was also, possibly, murder. Years in a prison like Coldbath Fields was a terrible fate for the guilty, but better than the gallows.

"You're sure about Hollister?" Scuff asked anxiously.

"I'm not completely sure," replied Crowe, leaning

forward in his chair and staring with a puzzled expression at the floor. "I don't want Hollister hanged for being the instigator of the whole plot. And Dolan is clever enough to make it turn out that way. As for Maddock, the watchman, he'd have to be alive to give us his story, so we don't know what it would be. Paul Dolan will almost certainly tell us whatever will save his father, and make Hollister take the brunt of the blame. After all, it all took place at Hollister's warehouse."

"But they were Dolan's goods," Scuff argued. "He could sell them up the river more easily than Hollister, if he's taking a share of them in return for his part in the insurance fraud. Does Hollister know anything about wools or silks? Does he have contacts who could keep their mouths shut? If these people got caught, they'd sell out Hollister in a heartbeat, but they'd be a lot more careful about implicating Silas Dolan!"

"I know." Crowe looked profoundly unhappy. "If we make a mistake, Silas Dolan might even manage to blame Hollister for it all, particularly the arson. And we can't forget that, when it comes to the law, the death of the night watchman is a hanging offense. Arson and insurance fraud are small crimes in comparison."

Scuff saw anxiety not only in Crowe's face, but in

his clenched hands and hunched shoulders. He did not want to be the one who brought this crisis to a head, in case he had to make a very difficult decision about what to report to whom, and have others pay for it. "Some operations have to be made, and the patient dies anyway," Scuff said slowly, looking for the right words. Something like the words Crowe had used when teaching Scuff about lancing boils, especially when they were on a part of the body too close to a vital organ or an artery. "When you have . . ." he started.

Crowe looked up and gave him a twisted smile. "I know. You're going to feed me back my own words. I have a knife in my hand, and I know enough of the boil to cut it, while I still have the chance. And it's not as if I had the excuse that it will cure itself if I leave it."

"No," Scuff agreed.

There was a long moment of silence. Nothing moved.

Scuff thought of several things to say, but he was sure that Crowe knew them already. Now that they both accepted Hollister's involvement, to pretend any longer would be not an evasion, but a lie.

Another fact that had to be taken into account was that Crowe had been asking about the shipment claimed for in the fire. However discreet he had been, he was putting himself and Scuff at risk. There would be whispers and suggestions; they couldn't be avoided.

"All right," he said at last. "I'll go in the morning. I'll tell Monk."

"No," Scuff said, speaking with an authority he did not really have. Crowe also knew Monk and his wife, but Scuff felt a special connection to the people who considered him their son. "I'll go . . . now."

"But you don't know the details," Crowe argued. "I have to go. And it's after midnight!"

"I know enough from what you've just told me," Scuff replied. "We need to let Monk know before there's even the smallest chance of the conclusion of your investigation getting back to Dolan. No one will tell Dolan tonight, it's too late. But I can tell Monk. I'll go—" He stopped. He had nearly said "home." But the clinic was his home now. "I'll go to Paradise Row now and tell him."

Monk and Hester lived in the optimistically named Paradise Row, which was up the hill a little from the Greenwich docks, 'round several corners, and next to a park full of trees.

Crowe stood up at the same time as Scuff. He opened his mouth to say something, then changed his mind.

"Go to sleep here by the stove," Scuff said, as if it

were an order. "I'll go and awaken Monk and then I'll come back here. If he wants to move quickly, they will need you to go with them, so be ready. Get some sleep," he said again. "If you go with them, which I suppose you will, I'll look after everything here."

Scuff walked over to where his coat was hanging on the row of hooks beside the door. "Prepare yourself," he said half over his shoulder. "Eat and rest." And then he went out into the starlit night.

*W*hen Crowe went up the river again, this time it was on a Thames River Police boat, with four strong men at the oars and William Monk in the stern, perched on the seat beside him. They were followed by another boat, carrying six more policemen. It rode over the surface of water so black it was almost sinister. There was no moon visible in the heavily clouded sky, but at least the wind was little more than a breath.

Monk sat silently. There were no more questions to ask. Scuff had given an explanation of the situation, and then Crowe had told him all he knew as they traveled up the river. Several things were no more than intelligent guesses, but it was enough to set this late-night operation into motion.

For Crowe, there was no point at all in wondering whether he had made the proper choice. What could he do but inform Monk? It had come to the point of no return. In fact, it had been since the moment he had told Scuff. This did not mean it was the right decision, or that whatever happened would not slip out of their control and end in a disaster they could not have foreseen. If the Dolans knew they were coming, it could end in a pitched battle with injuries . . . or worse.

And there was nothing to indicate that any of the goods would still be in some upriver warehouse . . . or even in Great Britain!

Crowe forced his attention back to the present. They were moving with surprising swiftness, considering that these boats were designed to cut through the water with a minimum load. Usually, there were no passengers.

Neither Monk nor Crowe spoke. There was nothing left to say, and they both lived more in their actions than their words.

For the first few miles, there were wharfs and docks, warehouses, cranes, and derricks, slipways for launching. Further along, there were shipbuilding yards, piled-up timbers. Every so often, they passed a steep wall with stone steps leading up to a landing. At the water's edge, at the foot of these steps, was where boats could pick up or land passengers.

They passed from deep water into the quiet, more domestic stretches of the river. There were houses with river-edge gardens, stretches of trees lining the banks. Villages had slipways for builders who made fishing boats and small ferries.

Crowe knew they were not far from their destination now. Even moving in the dark, the outlines of warehouses and derricks were familiar. He could see lights on the shore, some of them moving, as if somebody had seen them coming. It was good they had riding lights! Of course they did. Everyone did, for their own safety, as well as that of other people. He wondered if they were recognizable by them.

Monk's men shipped their oars and the boats drifted silently. Crowe closed his eyes and imagined the lost cargo. Much of it had certainly been sold long ago, or moved, but perhaps there were still bolts of silk and wool, and the white furs. The furs were unique, and it would not be difficult to prove they came from the collection of luxury goods that had been claimed as a loss with the insurance company.

The boats behind them also shipped their oars. The darkness and shifting shadows made judgment of distance difficult, but Crowe sensed they were fast closing on the wharf and the shore.

A shout echoed across the water. The wharf was now visible in the darkness, but only because of a guide light at the furthest point from land.

Suddenly, the black wharf rose over them like the bow of a battleship.

Monk tapped the shoulder of the oarsman nearest to them and gestured. The man put the oar back in the water, and with considerable skill, guided the boat toward the steps, which were visible only in the single riding light attached to their own boat.

Monk gave the signal to go ashore, ordering one of the oarsmen to stay where he was. If they needed to make a quick escape, the boat would be ready for them.

Monk stood, climbed out of the boat, and then swiftly, almost silently, moved up the steps. Crowe went after him, clutching the single rail to stop himself from losing his footing on the slimy wood, worn thin and smooth by countless feet over generations of men climbing up from the water.

At the top, they kept low. Dark as the sky was, a

black silhouette could still be seen by anyone watching, with eyes accustomed to the ice-cold winter's night.

Crowe wondered if there was anyone watching their stealthy arrival. It was far from daylight, with no light promised for several hours. With a start, he suddenly remembered that today was Christmas Eve!

Monk held his hand up and stood motionless. They all listened. There was no sound but the faint murmuring of the water. No dripping, not even a sigh of the wind.

Twelve men trod silently across the wet wooden boards. They all carried bull's-eye lanterns, but not one of the lanterns was turned on.

They moved forward slowly, with Crowe following.

The place seemed deserted, but Crowe figured that there must be a night watchman nearby, someone whose responsibility was to guard against fire or theft. After all, there could be highly valuable goods stored inside. Was this a repository for storing fragile things, valuable objects such as paintings, other works of art . . . or goods that were supposed to have been destroyed in a fire, and had to be concealed from even the most casual observation?

One of the policemen was a highly skilled lock pick. Crowe watched him work rapidly and in silence, while another man held up a bull's-eye lantern to give him light, sheltered from view by his own body. It took perhaps one minute before the lock pick stepped back and gestured for Monk to open the door.

As they entered, a thought ran through Crowe's mind. They would have to be quite lucky, so long after the fire, for any goods to still be hidden away and not be dispersed to points unknown. He shook the idea away. It would make sense to keep some of the goods, those that were most identifiable, locked up until no one remembered their existence.

With one policeman left behind as a lookout, the others went inside. Crowe assumed that at this hour, and so close to Christmas, all the warehouse workers were at home sleeping, surrounded by holiday spirit.

The men moved silently into the huge space. It seemed to be less than half full of crates and containers, but it took all the men to search for the bales of goods they hoped would be here.

After inspecting nearly every possible corner and surface of the warehouse, a murmuring sound of discovery reached Crowe's ears. He rushed over to where several of the policemen were clustered, Monk among them. Hidden under old tarps were seven bales of silk, three bales of fine wool, and one extremely large bundle more heavily wrapped than the others. Monk accepted a pocket knife from one of his policemen and carefully cut the cord holding it together. Inside were some fur stoles, each one individually packed to preserve the suppleness of the skins and the sheen.

Crowe moved closer. He caught his breath. One of the stoles was identical to Ellie's.

A policeman ran his fingers over the fur. "Poor wee beastie," he said softly.

Crowe felt a shaft of emotion run through him. These animals had been killed, not to feed people, but for the beauty of their pelts, to satisfy the fashion wishes of the wealthy. His mind flashed back to Ellie at her father's house, standing there and showing him the fur Dolan had given her. How had she felt, wearing the skin of an animal? For no reason he could think of, he saw Mattie curled up on the blanket on the floor, and the tiny kitten asleep beside her, its nose close to her cheek.

It was at that moment that lanterns suddenly appeared, illuminating the part of the floor near the door. One of the River Police started to shout, but the cry died in his throat.

Crowe spun round. Paul Dolan was standing at the edge of an open space on the warehouse floor, with a pistol in his hand. It was pointed at one of the policemen. Behind him, other shadows took shape. Crowe hoped they were Monk's men, ready to close in on Dolan, and guessed there were at least eight or nine of them. But as they became visible, he saw that they were not from the police. So, Paul was here, ready to fight, no doubt sent by his father.

All movement stopped.

And then a policeman stepped forward and announced himself, his voice ringing through the cavernous space. "Sergeant Olsson, Thames River Police! Put the gun down, sir."

Paul stood there, the gun gripped firmly, and now aimed at Olsson.

"There are ten of us here," said Olsson, as if speaking to a man who was neither armed nor dangerous. "Are these your goods?" He gestured toward the biggest stack closest to them.

Paul hesitated.

Sergeant Olsson smiled bleakly. "If they aren't, then what are you doing here? And if they are, maybe you'd like to tell us where you got them from?"

"You don't look like the police to me," Paul answered. And then he smirked. "Oh, River Police, yes?" He said this as if they were of lesser caliber than city police. "Of course, when you are all dead, we'll take your uniforms and your badges, and then you'll look like common thieves. Or even tramps coming out of the cold. But how were we to know? We caught you here, didn't we? And we thought you might be arsonists. With all that trouble before, one has to be careful. Everybody knows that!" He smiled as if the thought amused him.

Monk stepped forward, now clearly out of the shadows. "A dozen tramps?" he said incredulously. "Planning another fire, are you? Burn us all to death? Like you burned the night watchman in Hollister's warehouse? That's a hanging matter. Perhaps that wasn't you . . . maybe it was your father?" His face looked strange and bleak in the light of the bull's-eye lanterns.

Crowe stared at Monk and saw the strength of his bones, curiously ageless in this unnatural light.

Paul hesitated, as if suddenly uncertain how to act.

There was a slight shuffling sound in the darkness.

No one moved.

Crowe looked around. How many men were actually in this barn of a place? Eighteen? Twenty? Was this mischance? Or had Monk and his men walked into a trap? He knew that the River Police were like any others, in that they did not carry firearms, only truncheons. He wondered if Paul was the only man present who had actually killed a man. If, in fact, he was the one responsible for the death of Maddock. But then, of course, there was Monk, whom Crowe was certain had killed. He knew this only because he had been told in confidence.

He looked around the vast space. Where was Silas Dolan? Surely he was here, too, in the shadows. How many men had he killed? None? Half a dozen?

There was a soft sound, as if a bale of fabric was sliding from its position above Dolan's head. Dolan glanced up just as it teetered on the edge of the tall stack where it was positioned, then he moved sharply sideways, raising his arm to ward off the impact. The bale landed inches away from him, hitting the floor with hardly a sound. He threw himself into the shadows, the gun still gripped in his hand.

Crowe looked up, expecting to find a policeman on top of the bales, ready to hurl them as weapons. At that height, and out of sight, whoever was there held a distinct advantage.

The next moment, another policeman broke from the shadows, dragging Paul with him, then striking him on the arm so hard that the gun flew out of his hand and landed on the floor.

Monk dived for it, while Crowe swiveled 'round just in time to avoid a blow to the side of his head.

Within seconds, they were all in a pitched fight. Other men came out of the darkness, and still more shadows moved, so that it was impossible to tell at first whether they were Dolan's men or River Police.

Someone emerged from behind a large stack of bales and moved forward. It was Silas Dolan, a revolver in his hand. He raised it and shot at Monk, just as another bale was dislodged. The shot went wild, the bullet striking a lamp. Glass exploded, shards finding their way into the arms and faces of anyone standing within range.

Chaos erupted.

Crowe tried to follow what was happening. In the frenzy around him, he saw Monk shoot at least one of Dolan's men, using the revolver he had snatched from the floor. He turned just in time to stop one of those men from striking him.

Memory washed over Crowe, scenes from his past that he had almost obliterated from his mind. He was a young man at sea, going anywhere, engaging in dockside brawls in foreign ports, fights when he had to watch for knives, fists, boots, anything used to defend or attack.

He had little idea how long this melee continued. There were shots, men yelling, bodies falling to the floor, some with visible patches of red spreading across an arm, a chest. Instinct came back and he remembered his old fighting skills, much as one remembers how to ride a horse. Once learned, it becomes second nature.

More shots rang out. Someone shouted. Bales tumbled from the tops of high piles, a few of them landing on men, others becoming defense positions, hiding whoever could get behind them.

The battle moved toward the main doorway, the dark of night still hanging over them. Crowe was driven forward, and then stumbled and fell over a body. The man was dressed in black, and appeared to be unconscious. At any other time, Crowe would have helped him, but after assuring himself that it was not one of the River Police, he left him where he lay and moved closer to the man he realized was Albert Hollister.

Why was he here? And what could Crowe say to him? Nothing that made any sense. There was nothing left to argue about. And, in a strange way, it was all very plain now . . . It all made sense.

Hollister turned to face Crowe, and recognition was instant in his face. "Did you bring them?" he accused, waving in the general direction of the last shout heard.

"Yes." Crowe did not want this confrontation, but neither would he lie about it. "If you stored these things here, and then helped Silas Dolan claim the insurance . . . and left the night watchman to burn—"

"I didn't!" Hollister shouted, fury in his voice. "I owed him. I had to agree to store his property in my warehouse, and I had a pretty good idea someone in his pay lit the fire." His voice cracked. "He told me that Ellie's life was the price I had to pay if I refused to help them. What could I do?"

Crowe had no idea whether to believe him or not.

Someone rushed to within ten feet of where they were standing, like a charging animal, ferocious. "Liar!" It was Silas Dolan. "Weakling!" He was pointing the gun at Hollister.

It would be Crowe next, and Crowe knew it.

Hollister let out a howl at the top of his lungs. "Stop him!"

There were two shots in rapid succession. The first bullet struck the wall just above Crowe's head, the second so close he heard it pass his ear.

And then a third shot.

Silas Dolan turned slowly, lost his balance, and fell to the floor. He did not move again.

Crowe froze for an instant and then dropped to his

knees, searching for a pulse in the motionless body. He found nothing.

He looked around, then stood up slowly and moved to the shelter of a large bale. Another shot rang out, and then an eerie silence closed in.

Seconds later, there was a rush of movement. Two more shots. Scrabbling feet, and then a bale fell from a height and burst open. A voice Crowe did not recognize swore continuously.

And then he heard Monk's voice, loud and firm, ordering his men to move toward the door. Crowe moved with them, then felt the cold air from outside.

There were more shouts of anger and abuse. He saw several of the men from the River Police handcuffing men who were agitated and resisting.

Behind them, Monk was practically dragging Albert Hollister, his wrists in handcuffs, and his face twisted in rage.

Hollister suddenly lunged forward. A shot rang out and he slumped, his weight dragging Monk down with him.

In three strides, Crowe was on them.

Monk slowly stood.

There was one final shot.

Crowe felt an overwhelming pain in his shoulder. And then . . . nothing.

*I*t seemed an endless night. It had been dark since a little after four in the afternoon, and it would not be light again until around eight this morning. Today was Christmas Eve!

Scuff lay in bed, silence all around him. He would have to be up well before daylight. Mattie would be awake by then, and the kitten certainly would be, too. Like any other baby, the furry little thing spent her time eating, sleeping, playing and exploring, and being immensely more mobile than any human infant.

Scuff knew he must sleep. If any cases came to the clinic, he needed to be wide awake, his attention sharp. He closed his eyes, but knew that he wouldn't sleep, his mind filled with possibilities of challenges awaiting him, even disasters. What if someone died because he did not know what to do? And where was Crowe? Had they found the goods? Were they able to get there and back safely?

He woke up with a start, sitting upright in bed. During his thoughts, he had fallen back asleep. Now someone was beating on the clinic's door! He grabbed his trousers and a sweater and pulled them on as he moved, knowing his way in the dark. It was lighter in the

187

kitchen, not from daylight but from the lamp they always kept burning, even before Mattie came. Sometimes emergencies happen during darkness as well as day.

The banging was still going on. He made his way to the door and opened the bolts, then turned the handle. Before he could pull the door wide, it was pushed in from the outside. It was pitch-dark on the street, but the first man in was carrying a bull's-eye lantern that threw a dim light over the area. And then Scuff realized that there were at least half a dozen men, the light showing only shapes. The man holding the lantern tilted it just enough to reveal that it was William Monk.

A shard of fear pierced Scuff. These men were carrying a body, and it was Crowe! His face was ashen, with blood covering his neck, chest, and one shoulder.

It was impossible to see the wound, or judge how serious it might be. For a moment, Scuff felt light-headed, a roaring in his ears.

Someone reached round him and pulled the door wide open, and Crowe was carried inside.

Scuff came to life. He led them into the kitchen. Not only was there more light here, but this room was the clinic's only source of hot water. The big pan on the stove was full. Scuff lit the stove and slid the pan over the flame.

Monk's face was haggard with strain, anxiety, and perhaps grief for this man who had helped Scuff so much. In the yellow lantern light, the shadows made his face even more dramatic, accentuating the weariness, the deep emotions, the stronger flash of silver at his temples.

With the shock of surprise, Scuff realized how very deeply Monk cared. This was a test of so much, not only of police skills. Had they found the goods that were supposed to have been burned? Could they prove the case of arson and murder against Hollister and Dolan? What would happen to Ellie? It made Scuff wonder if he was really learning to be a doctor, or was he just dreaming, and still no more than a mudlark at heart.

But at the moment, there was only one question that really mattered: Could he save Crowe? A shoulder wound should not be fatal, but he was so pale, and still unconscious. If he did not treat the wound properly, it could turn gangrenous, and within days, at best, his friend and mentor could lose his arm. What was a surgeon with only one arm? And there was another possibility, far worse: he could die.

Monk was still staring at him. "Get the bullet out and stop the bleeding. Tell us what to do to help."

Scuff forced himself to think what Crowe would do if their roles were reversed. "Put him on the table," he directed, pointing to the large table they kept for those few occasions when they had to operate, and the far more frequent occasions when they needed to examine a person, which was made easier if they were lying down.

They lifted Crowe gently onto the table. "And take that coat off," directed Scuff. "Cut it off, if you need to. Don't move the shoulder at all."

He turned his attention to putting together all the instruments he might need, and making sure they were where he could reach them easily. He also produced bandages, alcohol to sterilize everything, and thread and needles for closing the wound.

He crossed to the cupboard and started to take out everything he would need. A small hand suddenly appeared, removing squares of sterilized cotton.

He turned and saw Mattie crouching beside him, her eyes wide, soft and frightened.

"We got somebody hurt?" she asked.

Should he tell the truth? A lie now might always be there, hanging over them like a dark cloud. "Yes," he answered. "I'm afraid it's Dr. Crowe." He saw the color leave her face. "So, we've got to be very careful," he went on. "Can you help me?"

She looked at him as her eyes pooled with tears. "Is he going to die?"

"No," Scuff said firmly. "Not if we get on with it and do it right. Will you thread some more needles for me, please? We'll cut the thread to various lengths and you can hand them to me when I ask you. Can you do that?"

She nodded very slowly.

"Good." He turned to the box holding the very fine gut. As he gathered his instruments, he saw how she very carefully threaded one of the needles. It took her a moment, but the triumph in her face was worth it.

"Right," he said. "Now do all these for me. We'll need them sometime soon."

He had everything prepared. The men were waiting for him. It was all as ready as it could be. This part he had to do alone. If he did it badly—if he forgot anything, missed anything—it could cost Crowe his arm . . . or his life.

He walked over to the table. After making sure that Crowe was still unconscious, he inspected the wound— the policemen had cut off Crowe's jacket and shirt.

Crowe's shoulder was still bleeding, but the blood was beginning to clot.

Crowe was cold to the touch. Too cold. Scuff felt for a pulse and for a moment found nothing. Panic grew inside him. He was too late. The wound was deeper than it looked. Somehow, it had hit an artery. They had taken too long getting him down the river. And then a warm gush of blood touched his hands. Thank God! If Crowe was bleeding, then he was still alive!

Scuff knew that he must find the bullet quickly and remove it. He gave a silent prayer that it was still in one piece, and not in fragments that could cause multiple tears in tissue and damage an artery. He had never prayed before. He wasn't certain that there was a God, in spite of Hester insisting that there was. Nevertheless, he prayed, just in case.

He pushed gently against the wound and another gush of blood appeared. There was something dark embedded in there; he hoped it was the bullet. But was it intact?

He took the forceps and inserted them carefully, but it was difficult to take hold of the object. After three attempts, he was finally able to work the object gently until it was loose. He gave one last, gentle tug and it slipped out easily. As he had hoped, it was the bullet, and it was in one piece. He dropped it into a bowl and tried to inspect the wound, but there was too much blood. He understood the urgency to clean it, repair the vessel, and close it quickly.

It took Scuff a long moment to find the precise source of the bleeding. When he pinpointed it, he probed to determine how to proceed. He needed to study the wound slowly, with care. A mistake could be fatal. He wished Hester were here! This wasn't some stranger, this was Crowe! Crowe, who trusted him.

He looked at Mattie, who was watching him. There was such hope in her face, such trust. He did not want people to trust him like this—he did not feel worthy.

"Please hand me that swab," he said, pointing at the cotton wool in the dish just beyond his reach.

Mattie picked it up with her fingertips and passed it to him, then reached for another, in case he needed that, too.

Scuff felt the men watching him, Monk among them. He nearly asked Monk to fetch Hester, but there was no time. He would have to do this on his own.

He took a deep breath, and let it out. There was no time to delay, to weigh one approach against another.

He could see one end of the blood vessel. Now he must find the other. *Calm down! It must be here.* He had watched Crowe perform similar operations, and tried to recall exactly what he had seen. Not in diagrams, but in real flesh.

The area was slippery with oozing blood.

Uncertainty beset him. At first, he was sure he had control, then he didn't. He told himself, *This is it; no, it isn't; yes, it is!*

Monk stepped closer. "What can I do?"

"Wash your hands in that spirit," Scuff said, indicating the container. "And then hold this in place for me." He handed Monk a sterile cloth and showed him where to apply it.

Monk looked at Scuff once, as if verifying that he was following instructions. When Scuff nodded, he turned his full attention to the wound.

Scuff worked carefully, one needle stroke at a time, using the finest thread to ease the wound closed.

"Another needle, please," he asked Mattie. It was handed to him immediately. "Thank you," he murmured.

Time seemed endless, each minute like an hour. Had he stretched the thread tightly enough? Too tightly? Was that ooze of blood there before?

He worked as quickly as he could. He reached for another needle from Mattie, then he swabbed the wound again and waited. There was very little bleeding. He needed to finish before Crowe regained consciousness. The pain would be appalling. The thought caused a cold bolt to shoot through Scuff. Crowe was going to wake up, wasn't he?

He introduced the last few sutures, careful to create a scar that would be neat and, in time, barely visible.

He was finished. There was nothing more he could do now. He stepped away from the table, and realized that he was cold, and at the same time covered in sweat.

Light was showing through the window, the first light of dawn.

"Is he going to be all right now?" Mattie asked soberly.

Scuff told the truth. "I hope so."

One of the men from the River Police came toward him, holding out a mug of steaming tea. "Here," he said quietly. "You look like you need it. You did a good job."

The tea was hot, and Scuff sipped it carefully. "Thank you," he said after several mouthfuls.

He looked round the room. There seemed to be a lot of people there, but he guessed they were all Monk's men from the River Police. He didn't know most of them. "Would you help me carry him to his bed?" he asked no one in particular.

"Is it all right to move him?" one of them asked. "The stitches won't come undone?"

"No," Scuff said with confidence, although he was thinking the same thing.

"'Course not!" Mattie said, and so firmly that Scuff knew she, too, was afraid.

His mind suddenly flashed to the little doll he had bought for her, and how pleased she would be to receive it. He glanced at her trusting face. She was family.

Ten minutes later, Crowe was in his bed, with Mattie sitting beside him and Rosie in her lap. Both child and kitten seemed to be watching him, as if making certain he was all right. She told Scuff she would fetch him if Crowe seemed to be doing poorly, or when he opened his eyes.

Scuff returned to Crowe's room several minutes later. Mattie was holding a feather under Crowe's nose . . . to make sure he was breathing.

Back in the huge kitchen, Scuff sat with a second mug of tea. "What happened?" he asked, looking at Monk.

Monk told him briefly about the discovery of the fabric and the furs. He described the ambush by Silas Dolan and his men. "Silas is dead," he said, "and we've arrested the entire gang, young Paul included."

Scuff nodded, but said nothing.

"And Hollister . . ."

Scuff's eyes widened. "Please don't tell me . . ."

"He's wounded, but alive," said Monk.

"I'm sure you'll be charging Paul Dolan with arson," he said. "And Hollister, too? But what will happen to Ellie?" He knew this would matter intensely to Crowe. When he awoke, Scuff wanted to be able to tell him some good news. "I'm sure she wasn't aware of any of this!"

"I don't know what will happen to her," Monk replied quietly. And then he described the scene, the pandemonium, and how Hollister had been shot. "Some of my men took him to a hospital near the wharf. He'll make it, but it won't be easy."

"Why didn't you take Crowe to the same hospital?" Scuff asked. "It was a risk to lose that time and bring him here."

Monk gave him a wry little smile. "He was just conscious enough to insist on being brought here. Stubborn, he is!"

Scuff was confused, and it showed in his face.

"He said you'd know what to do."

Scuff gave a little smile, and then he shrugged. At the same time, he felt a swell of pride. If Crowe requested this, then he must trust him. After a moment, Scuff said, "Poor Ellie. Does she know?"

"We sent Hooper to tell her."

Scuff knew that Hooper was Monk's second in command, and one of the best men Scuff had ever known. He was almost as good as Monk himself.

"Her father was involved in the fraud," Monk said. "I don't know if he was involved in the fire. Silas Dolan is dead, and young Dolan will go to prison for a long time. It's pretty clear that Hollister was a pawn."

It was a lot for Scuff to take in in these few moments. "Crowe will worry about Ellie."

Monk smiled. "Tell him not to worry. We'll make sure she isn't blamed for any of this. And if her father tells us everything he knows, we might be able to keep him out of prison."

That evening, the outside door swung open, letting in a blast of cold air. It was nighttime, which surprised Scuff. The hours had flown by and outside was as black as a coal mine. Hooper came in. He gave a brief nod to Monk. With him was Ellie Hollister. She was wrapped in an oilskin coat that was so large on her that it dragged on the floor. She went straight to Scuff.

"I think Crowe's going to be all right," Scuff said, before she could ask.

"Thank you." Her eyes filled momentarily with tears of relief. "He will be so proud of you."

"How's your father?" Scuff asked.

"I just left him," she said. "He's in pain, but the doctor says he'll recover."

Mattie walked over to Ellie, and shyly took her hand. "I'm looking after Dr. Crowe," she said.

Ellie relaxed and, at last, she smiled. "Thank you," she said to Mattie, and then she turned to Scuff. "Do you think I could see him?"

When Scuff nodded, Mattie tugged on her hand. "Come with me," she said, and then led Ellie out of the kitchen.

Scuff followed after them. He needed to know how Crowe was doing.

Crowe was lying exactly where they had left him. His face was so pale it was nearly white, but his eyes were open.

Mattie took charge. "You're going to be all right," she said firmly. "Scuff stitched you all up, after he took the bullet out. I fixed the needles for him."

Scuff looked at Crowe carefully. He placed his fingers on Crowe's wrist. His pulse was regular, and quite strong.

"You did a good job," Crowe said softly, directing his comments to both Scuff and Mattie. His voice was dry in his throat. "A very good job. Thank you." And then he turned his gaze to Ellie. "Your father?"

"Father will recover. There may be a few problems, but we'll deal with them. What is most important is that he'll cooperate with the police. I'll see him again later on."

"And you?" asked Crowe. "How are you?"

"I'm no longer a hostage to Silas Dolan's threats. I wish I could feel sadness that he's dead, and that Paul is under arrest. Instead, I feel free." Crowe smiled at her reply.

Scuff observed, and then found his own voice, although it was a little husky. "You taught me well," he said to Crowe. A sudden smile appeared on his face. "Now you have to stay put for a while, and do as you're told."

Crowe smiled, and looked beyond Scuff to where Ellie was standing.

She came and sat on the edge of the bed. "Are you really all right?" she asked anxiously. "They say that

Silas Dolan shot you." Her eyes welled with tears, but she ignored them. "If my father honors his word, there's nobody left to prosecute except Paul Dolan and his gang."

"I'm sorry your father was involved. I had hoped he would not be," Crowe said huskily. He was afraid for her, and it showed in his face.

"We'll sell the house," she said. "And then pay his debts. All of them. And then his name will be, at least in part, saved. It was part of the hold Silas Dolan had over him—to restore his fortune—but there is a better way."

"Where will you go?" His voice had an urgency, as if it was unbearable to imagine her leaving for some far-away place. Away from him . . . out of his life.

Ellie took a deep breath and bit her lip for a moment, then she looked at him as if she had just come to some inner conclusion. "I thought I would stay here." She gestured at the space around them.

"Here?" he repeated. "How could you possibly stay here?"

"It would be quite proper, you can be certain of that."

Crowe studied her face for a moment. "Ellie, you and I would know it was proper, but what about . . ."

"The rest of the world?" she asked. "Or just London?"

"No," he said. "I can't let you do that."

She looked at him, as if scrutinizing every feature of his face.

Crowe tried to discern what she was thinking, but nothing logical came to mind. When she finally spoke, he found himself unable to respond.

"It's all very acceptable, I assure you," she said. "That is, if you ask me to marry you."

Crowe closed his eyes. When he spoke, his voice was choked with tears. "I can't do that. I can barely feed myself, and this is no place for a lady."

She took a sharp breath, another, and then she looked away.

The way Crowe's face changed, Scuff knew he was holding back a powerful emotion. Losing Ellie would devastate him.

"It's very unladylike," Ellie said carefully, forcing every word. "But you leave me no choice."

There wasn't a sound in the room.

"So," she went on, "I must be the one to ask. Dr. Crowe, will you marry me?"

In the ensuing silence, Scuff was almost bursting with an impatience he could not contain.

Crowe tried to sit up, but could not. His head dropped back onto the pillow. "Ellie, what can I offer you? A poor doctor and a clinic that will never provide the kind of comforts so many society doctors enjoy. And no," he quickly added, "I could never be one of them. This is where I belong, where I'm needed." He shifted so that he was no longer looking at her, his eyes blinking hard. When he looked back at Ellie, she was smiling.

"Do you think so little of me that I expect wealth? Or any of those comforts my father insists I must have? If that's the case, I take back my offer."

Crowe looked long and steadily at Ellie, and then let out his breath. "Fine, you win."

"Meaning?" she asked.

"Yes," he said. "Yes, I will."

"Will . . . what?" She leaned so close their faces nearly touched.

"Marry you," he said, and then he smiled. "If you insist."

Scuff sensed that it must be close to midnight, and this the longest evening of his life. But the joy he was feeling now, the sense of truly belonging, brought tears to his eyes.

Suddenly, beyond the wind in the darkness, somewhere in the vast reaches of the city, church bells began to ring, peal after peal.

Crowe took Mattie's hand and then, releasing it, gave Scuff's arm a gentle squeeze. "Happy Christmas," he said huskily to everyone in the room. Scuff presented Mattie with the doll he had come across. She accepted it with glee.

Ellie leaned over and kissed Crowe, long and gently. "Happy Christmas," she replied.

## ABOUT THE AUTHOR

ANNE PERRY is the *New York Times* bestselling author of nineteen previous holiday novels, as well as the William Monk series, the Charlotte and Thomas Pitt series, the Daniel Pitt series, the Elena Standish series, five World War I novels, and a work of historical fiction, *The Sheen on the Silk*. She lives in Los Angeles.

anneperry.us
Facebook.com/AnnePerryAuthor

To inquire about booking Anne Perry for a speaking engagement, please contact the Penguin Random House Speakers Bureau at speakers@penguinrandom house.com.

ABOUT THE TYPE

This book was set in Century Schoolbook, a member of the Century family of typefaces. It was designed in the 1890s by Theodore Low De Vinne (1828–1914) of the American Type Founders Company, in collaboration with Linn Boyd Benton (1844–1932). It was one of the earliest types designed for a specific purpose, the *Century* magazine, because it was able to maintain the economies of a narrower typeface while using stronger serifs and thickened verticals.